Focus

the

crescent chronicles

ALYSSA ROSE IVY

ISBN: 1482061236
ISBN-13: 978-1482061239

OTHER BOOKS BY ALYSSA ROSE IVY

To Andrea and Samantha: Laissez les bons temps rouler

ACKNOWLEDGMENTS

As always, this book would never have been possible without the amazing support of my family. Grant, I appreciate your support and encouragement more than you will ever know.

Thanks to Jennifer Snyder for being there every step of the way. Thanks to Kris Kendall for a wonderful editing experience. Thank you Kristina Scheid for a great proofread.

Thanks to Tiffany, Heather, and Ana for the wonderful costume suggestions.

Thanks to all of my Tulane friends for making college so amazing that it inspired this story.

Thank you to all of the bloggers who have helped spread the word about my books. And of course, a huge thank you to my readers for letting me share my stories with you.

CHAPTER ONE

"All right, I think that's everything." I flopped down on my new bed, sweaty and exhausted yet unbelievably excited.

"It's official... we're in college." Hailey mirrored me, sitting up on an elbow across the room. "Umm, you boys can go now." She made a shooing motion at the three large guys leaning against the wall under the air conditioning vent.

"Just like that, you're kicking us out?" Jared complained.

Hailey sat up, sitting with her legs crossed. "Oh wait, I forgot. Ground rules. Under no circumstances can you flirt, hook up with, or otherwise interact with any of the girls on this floor. Is that understood?"

Owen and Levi both laughed, the rules weren't for them.

"You can't tell me what girls I can hook up with." Jared ran a hand through his black hair.

"Yes she can. You are not making things weird for us." I crossed my arms over my chest, trying to make myself look more intimidating.

1

"And how are you going to enforce it?" Jared challenged.

"Do you even want to go there? Do you want us to tell every freshman girl you have an STD, or just our floor?" I threatened. "Don't test us."

"Okay, okay." He held up his hands in mock defeat. Knowing Jared, he was already trying to find a loophole. He wasn't one to step away from a challenge.

"Hey, Al, can I talk to you for a second?" Levi used his nickname for me instead of calling me Allie like everyone else.

"Uh, sure." I looked at him, waiting for him to continue.

"Alone."

Hailey glanced at me to gauge my reaction. I nodded. Levi was nothing if not persistent, so it was probably better to get the conversation over with.

"All right guys, time to help me buy my books." Hailey walked towards the door with Owen and Jared on her tail.

"You're lucky you are my sister or you'd be dead right now." Owen touched the molding above the door on his way out.

"What's your excuse, Jared?" I called after him.

He grunted, and Hailey laughed. She loved her new power over the guys now that they were willing to do anything to keep me happy. They left the room. Jared slammed the door behind him.

It was the first time Levi and I had been alone in a room together since the night that changed my life forever—or really the morning after.

I sat up on my bed and Levi took it as an invitation to sit next to me. I could tell he was itching to touch me, but he knew better.

"So I was thinking we might get dinner tonight. Maybe Jacques-Imos?" His brown hair had grown out a little longer than when I first met him. I was tempted to tell him to get a haircut, but he'd probably enjoy that too much.

"Why would I go to dinner with you?" I smoothed out the light blue comforter.

"Why wouldn't you? I'm really glad you agreed to let me help you move in. I've missed you so much."

"Why would the fact that I was interested in using you for your physical labor, equate with us going out?"

"Come on! I just spent the better part of the day lugging boxes of your stuff up three flights of stairs." He crossed his arms, which only accentuated the muscles underneath his shirt. Carrying boxes couldn't have been too hard for him.

"And I appreciate that, but it still doesn't change anything." I knew how cold I sounded, but he deserved it.

"Please, Al. You can't stay mad forever. It's just dinner. Or if you don't want to do dinner, let's go out later tonight." His gray-blue eyes pleaded with me, but I looked away before I could even be tempted.

"I can't do this. You're supposed to be giving me space."

"Space? I never agreed to that. What do you expect me to do? I'm dying here." He put his head in his hands. It was still weird to see Levi look so defeated.

"Why? Because you can't handle going a few weeks without getting some?" Out of habit, I tugged at the ring that was at the center of all of my problems.

"I waited a lot more than a few weeks for you the first time around." By the expression on his face, he probably regretted the words instantly. "This isn't about sex and you know it."

"Then what is it about?"

"Us. We are so good together, let's give it another chance." His voice was low and husky.

I closed my eyes, trying to ignore the dull ache inside that made me want to reach out and touch him. He took advantage, but really I left myself open.

His lips met mine as his arm wrapped around my shoulder, turning me toward him. A voice in my head told me to cut him off, but I ignored it. He pushed to deepen the kiss, and I let my resistance fall away. He leaned into me, moving me so I was lying down. I felt his weight shift on top of me, his lips moving to my neck and trailing downward. I snapped myself out of it. Kissing Levi was a really bad idea.

"Stop!" I pushed against his chest. He didn't respond at first, but he reluctantly moved to let me sit up. "What the hell was that?"

He grinned. "Don't say you didn't want that."

"Don't look so proud of yourself. It's never happening again." I straightened my hair out with my fingers, trying to get rid of the evidence.

"So about tonight?"

"What about it?" I snapped.

"What do you want to do?" He sat up, still looking way too proud of himself.

"I'm going to a party with Hailey. She says all the freshman will be there."

"Please tell me you aren't talking about Disorientation."

"Yeah, I think that's what it's called."

He shook his head. "No way. You're not going!"

As if on cue, the door started to open. "Are you two decent in there?" Jared yelled obnoxiously.

I groaned. "Of course, we are."

Hailey and the boys pushed into the room.

"Are you sure about that?" Owen asked.

I probably blushed wondering what evidence still existed. I followed his gaze and realized my tank top was pulled up on one side. Levi pulled it down before I could, letting his hand graze my skin in the process. The goose bumps that formed were completely coincidental—or so I told myself.

I stood up, needing to put distance between us. "That was fast."

"Yeah, we heard the line was out the door and came

back. We'll have to try again later."

Jared rolled his eyes. "Not with our help."

Levi turned his attention to Hailey. "Al seems to think you two are going to Disorientation tonight. Where would she have gotten the idea that that was acceptable?"

"Why wouldn't we go?" Hailey took a seat on her desk chair.

"You have got to be kidding." Owen slumped down on the floor, fanning himself with his shirt. "You really think Levi is going to let Allie go to a party like that?"

"One of the only good things about living in this dorm is being close to the frat houses. We're not missing this party." Hailey made no secret about how mad she was about living in an all-girl dorm.

"Then we'll go with you." Levi stood up.

"No way. Absolutely not!" Hailey yelled. "We want to have lives. We can't have them if you are hovering over us all the time."

Anger built up inside me. I was tired of people talking about me like I wasn't there. "Why would Levi have any say over what parties I go to? I can do what I want."

"Fine. You want to go to that party? Go." A sly grin crossed Levi's face.

"Uh oh. What are you planning?" I sighed in frustration.

"Why would you assume I am planning anything?" he said with mock innocence.

"Because you never give in that easily."

"Well, I guess you'll have to wait and see." Levi took a step toward me, kissing me quickly before I could react. "See you around, Al." He winked before heading towards the door.

Jared and Owen got up to follow him. "Try to stay out of trouble, Hailey," Owen warned as they filed out.

"Yes, *Dad!*" Hailey yelled back even though the door had already slammed shut. "My brother has to be the most annoying person on earth."

"Second. Levi gets the first place prize."

"What about Jared? I think he wins too."

I laughed. "Maybe they're all tied?"

"All right, let's call it a three-way tie."

***

"Oh my god. I figured it was going to be you!" The door burst open, and a small girl with her black hair pulled back into a bun ran into the room.

"Anne…hey." I put down the dress I was about to hang up in my closet.

"Hi, Anne," Hailey said carefully. We weren't sure how the girl who was supposed to be Hailey's roommate was going to react to the change in room assignments.

"So you decided to stay in New Orleans after all?" She moved into the room.

I nodded. "Yeah, I just wasn't ready to leave."

"I totally get that." She sat down on my bed. "So how did you two manage to get the rooms switched? I'm not mad or anything, I'm right next door, so we'll still be able to hang out a lot."

"Yeah? That's awesome. Hailey's dad called and was able to move things around. It turned out there was an extra spot on the floor."

"Okay, cool. My roommate seems nice, but really quiet." I couldn't quite suppress a smile. Quiet: the exact opposite of Anne. It would be an interesting combination.

"Great."

Anne picked up the orientation packet I had sitting on my bed. "Do you guys want to meet her? She's just sitting in there all alone."

"Yeah, definitely." I deliberated on what to bring with me, finally settling on just my keys, phone, and my newly minted Tulane ID. Thankfully, the photo had turned out well.

Anne led the way into her identically laid out room.

"Hey Tiffany, this is Hailey and Allie, our neighbors."

A girl looked up from putting books on the shelf above her desk. "Hi." She brushed her blonde hair off her shoulder.

"Hey, it's nice to meet you." I smiled.

She smiled back shyly, and I took a seat on Anne's bed.

"So where are you from, Tiffany?" I'd been really shy as a little kid and knew how tough it could be.

"St. Louis." She sat down on her desk chair, turning it to look at us.

"Oh cool. I've never actually been there, but I've heard good things."

Tiffany put a hand on the arm rest of her chair. "Where are you guys from?"

"I'm from New York, and Hailey's a local."

"A local? You're actually from New Orleans?"

Hailey laughed. "Yes. I know there aren't too many of us here."

"That must have been cool. But then again, growing up in New York City would be cool too."

"Oh, I'm actually from the suburbs. I probably should have been more specific." I crossed my legs.

Tiffany smiled. "I do the same thing. I'm from the suburbs too."

"Am I the only non-suburbanite here?" Hailey took a seat next to me on Anne's bed.

"I'm really from Jackson, but it's not exactly a bustling metropolis." Anne zipped up a suitcase and jammed it into her closet.

Hailey laughed. "Hey, there's nothing wrong with Jackson."

Anne smiled. "Says the girl from New Orleans."

"So do you guys want to go to a frat party tonight?" Hailey asked.

"Yes!" Anne answered excitedly.

Tiffany twisted the fabric of her t-shirt with her hands. "Thanks, but no thanks. I think I'll just stay back."

"No way, you have to come!" Anne said excitedly. I had to give her points for enthusiasm.

"How about you just think about it?" I suggested. "I kind of want to go explore for a bit. You want to come, Hailey?"

"Sure, I'll show you around."

"I'm going to finish unpacking." Anne kneeled down to pull out some towels from a box on the floor.

"Same here." Tiffany smiled shyly again.

"All right, we'll stop by later."

As soon as we were at the stairs, I told Hailey what was on my mind. "We have to get Tiffany to go with us."

"Definitely. I think she wants to, but she's nervous. We'll convince her." Hailey pushed open the door, and we headed out into the humid heat of August in New Orleans. "But I just have to say it one more time; I can't believe we're in college."

I laughed. "I know. It's going to be an awesome semester."

CHAPTER TWO

Anne took a step into the hallway just as we came out of our room. I locked the door behind us.

Anne bent down to fix the strap of her sandal. "You guys ready?"

"Yeah. Where's Tiffany?" I asked.

Anne gestured inside and smiled. "I think she's coming."

"Awesome." I peered into the room. Tiffany was staring at her reflection in the floor length mirror affixed to the wall next to her bed.

She turned from the mirror. "Are you guys sure I look okay in this?"

Tiffany was dressed like the rest of us in a short jean skirt and a tank top. "You look great."

We took the stairs, all giddy about the night. Even though I'd been to plenty of parties in my life, it felt different going to one as an actual college student.

We headed outside towards the noise of Broadway, the street that was home to all of the fraternity and sorority houses. I'd opted for my usual choice of flip flops, relieved when Hailey assured me party attire was casual at Tulane.

Floods of students moved all around us. The night was filled with laughter and shouting as groups of friends reunited and new students got ready for their first night out. I was unable to prevent a smile from plastering itself on my face—there was just this incredible feeling in the air.

"So where's this party again?" Tiffany asked.

"Don't worry, we won't be able to miss it," Hailey assured her.

She was right. Disorientation was at a frat house about four blocks down from where we exited campus. An old fire truck was parked on the front lawn, but Hailey led our group right up to the front steps. I wasn't sure what the truck was doing there, but since Hailey didn't bat an eye, I figured it was normal.

"Welcome, ladies." An attractive guy greeted us when we reached the front door.

"Hey." Anne grinned.

"Welcome to Alpha Omega."

"Thanks." I pushed past him inside.

The house was packed. I couldn't see anything through the sea of bodies. Loud music pulsated. I glanced behind me to make sure my friends were with me. Tiffany looked like she was ready to pass out, Anne was grinning, and Hailey just looked like Hailey.

We maneuvered our way through the crowd to the back bar area. "Hello, girls," a guy said as we finally pushed up to the bar. "Need a drink?"

"Definitely." Anne reached out her hand to take a plastic cup. Hailey intercepted it.

"No, we want the other stuff."

"This is the good stuff," the guy said quickly.

"Nope. Hold on a sec." Hailey turned around and grabbed a random guy by the arm and looked in his cup.

"We want the blue punch, not the red."

The guy smiled. "Someone taught you well."

"Yeah, myself. Can we have four cups of the blue,

please?"

"Sure."

We accepted the cups and walked away.

"What was that about?" I was impressed Anne had stayed quiet while Hailey negotiated. "Is there something in the red stuff?"

"Whenever they have two different vats of a drink you need to be careful. If nothing else, it's double the alcohol."

"And that is bad because...?" Anne put a hand on her hip.

"You can get drunk at these parties, but not trashed. Trust me, okay?"

"Thanks." Tiffany smiled before taking a tiny sip of her drink.

"No problem. This isn't my first frat party."

I loved being friends with Hailey.

With cups in hand, we moved outside. As hot as it was, the temperature dropped once we got out of the house.

"Hi there." I turned as a blond haired guy called out to me.

"Hi."

"Having fun?" He moved closer.

"Sure, but we just got here." I took a sip of the drink. It was too sweet, but otherwise okay.

"Nice." A few other guys joined him, likely noticing he'd struck up a conversation with our group.

"So, are you freshmen?"

"Yeah. What year are you?" Anne asked.

"Sophomores," his friend answered.

"Cool. So are you an Alpha Omega then?" I asked.

"Yeah. I'm glad you girls decided to come by."

"We wouldn't have missed it." Anne put a hand in the pocket of her dark, jean skirt.

"So what are your names?" the first guy started to ask.

"Allie? What are you doing here?" A brown haired boy wearing a collared shirt interrupted.

"Brandon? Wow, I forgot you went to Tulane."

"You two know each other?" the second guy asked, looking between us.

"We went to the same high school," Brandon explained. He looked completely different from the last time I'd seen him. He'd always been a little on the nerdy side—people had been surprised when he decided to go to school in New Orleans. "I didn't know anyone from your class was coming here."

"Yeah, this was last minute."

"Cool, cool. We'll definitely have to catch up."

I nodded. It was fun to see a familiar face. "Sure, that sounds good."

"Oh Brandon, this is Hailey, Anne, and Tiffany."

"Hi there." He didn't bother to introduce the guys who had been hitting on us.

I noticed Brandon checking out Anne. She didn't seem to mind it.

"It's a small world, isn't it?" One of the mystery guys asked.

"Definitely."

"I'm David, by the way." He held out his hand, and I accepted the handshake. "Do you need more to drink?" He looked into my nearly empty cup.

"Yeah, but make sure it's the same stuff."

He laughed. "There's nothing in the other punch. I promise."

Before I could respond, the guy from out front was whispering in his ear.

David paled. "Uh, sorry. I had no idea who you were." He backed away.

"Who I am?" I looked at Hailey for an explanation.

Hailey shook her head, and I knew this all had something to do with Levi.

I turned back to tell David not to worry but he was gone, as were his friends. Only Brandon remained.

"That was weird…" Tiffany trailed off.

"Weird isn't the right word," Hailey said bitterly. "Allie,

I think we need to have a chat with my brother and his friends."

"I was thinking the same thing." Levi had no right to interfere with my life like that.

"Can we come?" Anne asked.

Hailey and I looked at each other. She shrugged. "Sure, why not."

We finished our drinks, tossed the cups, and walked back through the house and out onto the front lawn.

"Are you sure they'll be there?" I asked as Hailey led us down the street. It's not that I really wanted to talk to those guys, but I didn't need Levi scaring away every male on campus.

"Yeah. I guarantee they'll be at Bruno's."

"All right." I tried to stay calm. Being mad at Levi was nothing new, but it didn't get easier. It's hard to deal with a guy who you both love and hate.

"But isn't Bruno's nineteen and up?" Anne asked. "I don't have a fake."

"You don't need a fake. It'll be fine." Hailey picked up her pace. She was clearly anxious to confront the guys.

"Nineteen and up, isn't that random?" Tiffany tugged on her skirt. I guessed it was shorter than what she usually wore.

"It's to keep freshman away." Hailey pulled her hair clip out, letting her long, red hair spill down her back.

I silenced a call on my cell from my mom. I'd have to call her back later. "Meaning us..."

"Technically." She smiled.

"Geez Hailey, what would we do without you tonight? First you tell us what drinks are safe at a frat party, and now you're showing us how to get into a nineteen and up bar." I nudged her arm.

"Shut up. You know you love me."

"Of course I do." Hailey and I had gotten even closer over the few weeks before starting school. I adamantly refused to go to anything Society related without her, and

I'd turned to her when I didn't think there was anyone else to trust. She was definitely the silver lining in all the craziness that was my life.

"IDs," the bouncer asked as we walked up.

Hailey looked him straight in the eye. "You don't really need them."

He laughed. "I don't? Come on."

I tensed, waiting for Hailey to use some Pteron power, but she did something even more surprising.

"I'll say it again. You don't really need our IDs, do you?" She leaned in closer to him.

He smiled. "All right Hailey. I'll let you in, but don't make it a habit of trying to sneak your friends in."

"I won't." She smiled again, flirtatiously. "My brother's here, right?"

"Yeah, they're in there somewhere." He blatantly checked Hailey out.

"Okay, cool."

"See ya." I turned around and he was definitely staring at Hailey's ass.

Anne and Tiffany looked to me for answers about what just happened, but I could only shrug. We followed Hailey in through the crowd.

***

"Hey girls, how was the party?" Owen laughed. We found all three of them sitting at a table with two girls, both blondes.

"It was great until you ruined it." Hailey's voice was cold. I was glad that I wasn't on the receiving end of her anger.

"You scared everyone away." I looked directly at Levi as I spoke. He leaned back in his chair, blatantly ignoring the blonde that was hitting on him.

"Oh, heaven forbid we stop guys from hitting on Levi's fiancé." Jared smirked, turning his attention back to the girl next to him.

"Fiancé? You're engaged, Allie?" Anne asked.

"Not exactly."

"You're wearing my ring." Levi looked back at me, challenging me to argue.

"I can't get it off." At least that part was true.

"So you broke off the engagement?" Tiffany looked back and forth at the two of us.

"We were never engaged." My fingers went to the ruby ring, more out of a habit than anything else.

"Then why are you wearing his ring?" Anne shifted her weight between her feet. I'm sure all of that walking in heels was wearing on her.

"It was a misunderstanding."

"A misunderstanding?" Anne arched an eyebrow.

Hailey thankfully moved the conversation off me. "We weren't the only ones you messed with. You screwed stuff up for our friends too." She gestured to Anne and Tiffany.

"Oh, hello there." Jared turned back to us again.

"The rules, Jared," I reminded him none to gently.

"Seriously?"

He'd already turned his attention to Tiffany. If I had any doubts before, I knew for sure that Jared went for the blondes. I figured that's where the girl currently pawing Levi came from.

"Are you going to join us or stand there all night?" Levi asked.

"There aren't enough seats available." I nodded toward the blonde closest to him.

She smiled, inching closer.

"My lap is always available." He grinned.

"That again? I thought we settled that a long time ago?"

"A lot's changed since then."

"Yeah, the offer is less appealing." My purse started to slip off my shoulder so I fixed it.

"You can go now." Jared didn't even look at the girls as

he spoke. He was still eyeing Tiffany.

"He doesn't want me to leave," the girl next to Levi cooed.

"Leave." Levi had moved his attention from my face to my legs. He wasn't even trying to hide it.

"Did you not hear the part about this being his fiancé?" Owen asked the girl.

"She said she wasn't."

"She is. It's just a game we're playing." Levi never took his eyes off me.

"What?" I took a deep breath, having this fight in front of my new friends wasn't smart. I already had a lot of explaining to do.

"But what she can't seem to understand is that I always win games."

In the weeks after tricking me into becoming his mate, Levi had tried a number of tactics to get me to forgive him. He tried being ultra-attentive and sweet, but we both realized how horribly that act worked. Next he tried to be aloof like he didn't care, but he crumbled after about a day. I wasn't just a girl to him. His position as the king of The Society depended on us being together. No pressure or anything.

"Fine. This is boring anyway." The two girls got up and walked away. I realized they were older than I originally thought, probably in their mid-twenties. I guess Jared didn't discriminate on age. I couldn't help but feel a little satisfied watching them leave. I might have been angry at Levi, but I didn't like the thought of him with anyone else—not that he could be. Giving me his family ring and consummating our relationship meant that if he as much as kissed another girl he could lose everything. I had to admit he was taking it pretty seriously.

"Now you don't have an excuse. Sit down." He gestured to the chair next to him.

We were still two chairs short. I looked behind me and noticed two empty chairs at the table next to us.

"Are you using these chairs?" I smiled at the guys at the table.

"Nope, want to join us?"

"No, she doesn't." Levi got up and pulled the two chairs over to his table, sitting down in one. My friends had taken the rest of the open seats.

"Thanks." I sat down. "Was that necessary?" I asked Levi.

"Yes," he whispered in my ear. "Very necessary. My mate wasn't going to be sitting at a table with a bunch of blood suckers."

"What?" I turned back to look at the guys. "Like literal blood suckers?"

He laughed. "Yes. I know how much you wanted to see real vampires."

I leaned into Levi without thinking. "I had no idea." I shivered.

"You can tell by their eyes. They all have a ring of color. It's nearly invisible unless you know what you're looking for." He put an arm around me and leaned in close. "But you're safe with me. Soon they'll all know to stay away from you."

"That doesn't help my friends." Thankfully, Jared was happily entertaining Tiffany. Anne seemed more than happy talking to Owen. I can't imagine what they would have thought of our conversation.

Levi shrugged. "It's you I worry about."

"How thoughtful," I grumbled.

He laughed. "So the party was a bust, huh?"

"You can't do that."

"Do what?" He took a sip of his drink.

"Tell everyone to stay away from me."

"Yes I can, and I will." He tightened his arm around me. "I'm giving you time, but we're going to be together, Al. Don't ever doubt it."

"Don't ever doubt I can change my mind in a second."

He tensed. "Okay, we'll back down, but don't do

anything stupid."

"I should be telling you that."

"You look great tonight."

Talk about a topic change. "Flattery isn't going to get you anywhere."

"That's the shirt you were wearing at the beach, isn't it?"

He was right. "You remembered what shirt I was wearing?"

"It's the first time I took your shirt off, of course I remember it." He leaned in so close, his lips brushed against my ear. "I also remember that black dress. I'll never forget that one." He so didn't need to be bringing up the one and only time we'd had sex.

I yawned. It had been a long day. "Okay, I'm kind of tired. Anyone else want to head back?"

"I'm ready." Tiffany gave me a sympathetic smile.

"Same." Hailey pushed back her chair.

"You coming, Anne?"

"Yeah. Nice meeting you, Owen."

Owen waved politely.

I went to stand up, but Levi put a hand on my arm. "One of these nights you're going to come home with me, and it's going to be soon."

"Keep telling yourself that. Night, guys." I waved.

As we passed the bouncer, he lightly touched Hailey's arm. "Find them?"

"Yeah, we found them."

Hailey had some explaining to do.

CHAPTER THREE

Microeconomics at nine a.m. on a Monday morning wasn't my idea of the best way to start the week, but when you register for classes last you don't have much choice.

Tiffany had a nine a.m. on the main quad too, so we walked together after breakfast. We left Hailey and Anne eating their cereal.

"Do you think it's going to be really different from high school?" She played with the straps on her backpack as we waited to cross the street.

I thought on it for a moment before answering. "I honestly don't know. I took loads of advanced placement classes in high school, but I don't think it's going to be the same."

She took a deep breath. "I think you're right. Okay, I need to relax."

I laughed. "You'll be fine. And remember, we're going to celebrate surviving our first day tonight."

"Pizza and chick flicks. It's a good motivation."

When we reached the quad, I started looking at the names on the buildings. I was about to give up on finding mine when I noticed the sign. "All right, Tilton Hall, this is me."

"I'm in Gibson. That's the big one, right?"

"Yup. Good luck." I'd been in that building once to meet with admissions, but I'd been more focused on not killing Levi or his father than anything else.

"You too."

I pushed my tote bag up on my shoulder and headed into the building. A burst of air conditioning hit me as soon as I walked in the door. After checking the number outside the door twice, I walked into the mostly empty classroom. I was expecting a huge lecture hall, but it wasn't all that big. The tables were on risers but didn't go too far up. I took a spot in the middle row, pulling out a notebook and a pen. I knew a lot of people would be using a laptop for notes, but I liked to do it the old fashioned way.

"Hi." A guy with brown hair took a seat next to me.

I looked around a little surprised he'd sit so close considering the class was empty but didn't really mind. "Hi. I guess we're early."

"I thought it might take me longer to find the classroom."

"Same."

The classroom started to fill, and I people watched for a while. I didn't recognize anyone else in the class, but that wasn't surprising because it wasn't very big.

"This seat's taken." A gruff voice interrupted. I turned around and came face to face with Jared.

"Really? There are plenty of seats." The guy wasn't so shy after all. Jared wasn't exactly an easy person to stand up to.

Jared moved a tiny bit closer. "Really, move it."

"Quit being an idiot, Jared, and sit down." I gestured to the seat on my right, the completely empty one. People were starting to stare.

"Fine." I didn't miss the glare he gave the still unnamed guy. I decided it was the perfect time to introduce myself.

"I'm Allie, by the way." I reached out a hand.

He accepted the handshake. "Brian. Nice to meet you."

Jared cleared his throat loudly. "So tell me, Princess, why'd you sign up for a nine a.m.?"

"I didn't have much of a choice."

"If you had let Levi take care of your registration, you could have had anything you wanted."

"I bet." I wasn't going to let Levi do me any extra favors. Getting me in last minute was plenty. "The real question is what are you doing here?"

"Just doing my job."

"Your job is to annoy the hell out of me?"

He leaned in closer. "No, but if that's a side effect, I don't mind. I'm protecting you. Levi would have signed up for it himself, but he needs certain credits still to graduate, so for two classes you're stuck with me."

"Two? What other class?"

"Some sort of chemistry thing. I don't know."

"Organic chemistry? You're taking organic chemistry with me?" I opened my notebook up to a blank page.

"Yeah, that's it. I'm not really into science so you better be ready to tutor me." He smirked.

"That's a joke, right? Please tell me that's a joke."

He was prevented from answering when the professor walked in.

Professor Talcom looked exactly the way I pictured a college professor would look. With graying hair and thick glasses, I had no doubt he knew a lot about economics.

He made a quick introduction and then started taking attendance. It didn't take long before he got to my name. "Allison Davis."

"Here." I raised my hand.

A guy and a girl in the front row turned around and looked at me.

Somehow I knew the stares I was getting had to do with Levi. I nudged Jared, but he ignored me, answering with a loud "here" when the name Jared Florence was called a few people later.

"If you could all take a look at your syllabus, we can get started."

I got a pen ready and watched the professor.

"As you can see, the majority of your grade will be determined by four exams and the final. There will be one short paper as well."

I made an asterisk next to the grading section.

Jared snickered.

I nudged him and he stopped.

After discussing the syllabus and his expectations for the semester, the professor let us out thirty minutes early. The same kids turned to look at me before leaving the classroom.

"See ya." Brian gave a small wave as he left.

"Bye."

I packed up my stuff, and I walked out with Jared. "They knew who I was, how?"

"Word's out Levi chose a mate and your name's circulating. Most people just don't know what you look like. They were checking out their future queen."

I checked my phone out of habit, but I didn't have any missed calls. "How can you say that so calmly? That's insane."

"Not really. I mean you wouldn't have been my choice, but evidently Levi wanted you."

"So, it doesn't faze you that I had no say in any of this?"

"Why should it? You obviously like him; I don't see why you're fighting so much." He dug into his bag without slowing down and pulled out a pair of sunglasses.

I groaned. "Forget it. I don't know why I asked."

"All right, so your next class is all the way in Newcomb. We can head over there now if you want." He put on his shades. He looked even more intimidating that way.

"You know where my next class is?"

"Of course. Owen's probably already there. Such an overachiever."

"Owen's in my French class?"

"What? Were you expecting Levi to be in intro French? He's fluent."

I don't know what I was expecting. "Well, I guess if it's going to be one of the three of you, I'd rather it be Owen."

"Don't let Levi hear you say that." He put a hand in the pocket of his cargo shorts.

"What? That I detest him the least?"

"That you'd rather spend time with him." With the sunglasses on, I couldn't get a good read on Jared's expression. I wasn't sure if he was seriously suggesting Levi would be annoyed about that.

"Why? What would Levi do?"

"You want me taking Owen's spot in all your classes? Because that's what would happen."

"Okay, keeping that statement to myself."

Jared chuckled. "Fast learner."

"But Levi wouldn't actually get the wrong idea, would he? I mean, obviously, I don't like Owen."

"He knows, but he still wouldn't like it. Trust me. If you haven't figured it out yet you're even dumber than I thought, but Levi is really possessive of what's his."

"Stop." I grabbed Jared's arm.

"Stop what?" He turned toward me as people stepped around us.

"Referring to me as his. I'm not his. I don't belong to anyone."

Jared picked up my hand, pointing at the ring. "This ring says otherwise. You're his."

I tugged at the ring. "You know I'd take this thing off if I could."

"Shh, keep it down." He looked over his shoulder.

"What?"

"Okay, you not living with Levi is one thing, but trying to explain to the underlings that you're not even with him right now, isn't cool. Got it?"

"Underlings?"

"Yeah, got a problem with the terminology?"

"Yes. It's disrespectful. God knows what you say about me when I'm not around."

He laughed. "Is that a joke?"

"No."

"I might be Levi's friend, but that doesn't mean I'd ever get away with bad mouthing his mate. You don't get how important you are, do you? Everything will make sense eventually."

"That's real helpful."

"'I know I am."

I groaned.

"Okay, this is Newcomb, you're on the second floor." We'd reached another quad of sorts. I knew my dorm was right on the other side of it.

"Thanks for the delightful conversation."

"Don't mention it. See you later."

"What, no door to door service?"

"Your next chaperone is right there."

I looked over my shoulder to see a smiling Owen. "Chaperone? I thought you were my bodyguards."

"Bodyguard, chaperone, take your pick." He pulled down his sunglasses for a moment so he could catch my eye before replacing them and walking off.

***

My French professor didn't use a word of English. I'd pulled myself through Spanish in high school, and I thought French would be a nice change of pace. Five minutes into the first class and I regretted my decision. I was done for.

"You okay?" Owen asked as we filed out of the classroom.

"I have absolutely no clue what our professor said

today."

He laughed. "Really? You've never taken any French?"

"No. Have you? Aren't we in a level one class?" I glanced at my workbook, dreading my first homework assignment.

"Yeah, but I know some French, just not super well."

"Oh. Damn. I'll have to get some help from Hailey."

Owen held open the door for me. "Hailey? Good luck with that."

"What?" I looked at him.

"Hailey's great and all, but teaching isn't her strong point. But you know who would be really good at helping you?"

"Don't say it."

"Levi." Owen grinned. "He's the best tutor you could find."

"Forget it. I'll figure it out on my own." The last thing I needed was to ask for tutoring from Levi.

"Suit yourself." He shrugged. "Are you going back to your dorm?"

"Yeah, I'm done with classes for the day since I don't have lab this week."

"I know."

I ignored how smug he was about all of this. Of the three guys, Owen was the most tolerable.

"It's only eleven so I have an hour before I meet Hailey for lunch, so yeah I think I'll go back to my room."

"Cool. Have a good one, Allie."

"Thanks, you too."

"Tell my sister hi."

"I will."

I looked over my shoulder before I walked into my dorm and saw Owen still standing there watching me. If they were being so careful today, why weren't they at other times? That's when it hit me—they probably were. I was probably always being watched. Thank goodness, I lived with Hailey. At least they didn't have to watch me sleep.

CHAPTER FOUR

Jared hadn't been exaggerating. I had a Pteron in every class with me. The only break from the guys I got was my Freshman seminar. I'd been able to get into the same one as Hailey. With Jared in Econ and Organic Chem, and Owen in French, I knew it would be Levi waiting for me in Art History on Tuesday morning. He leaned against the outside of the building, holding two cups of coffee. "Good morning, love."

"Hi, Levi." I accepted the coffee, knowing he would have gotten it right, two Splendas and no cream. "Thanks."

"No problem. You ready for class?"

"Sure, let's go."

I followed Levi as he picked two seats in the center of the room. He got the seats right. I hated sitting in the back or front.

"These okay?" Levi asked as he sat down.

"Perfect, thanks." I put my bag down on the floor and took out a new, blue notebook and pen.

He smiled. "Did you just thank me for the second time this morning?"

"Yes, but don't let it go to your head."

"Don't worry. I will."

I shook my head.

Levi sat down next to me, putting an arm around the back of my chair.

"So how was your first day yesterday? Was it all you wanted it to be?"

I turned to glare at him. "Don't you already know? Didn't your two goons fill you in?"

"My goons?" He laughed. I hated how much I loved that deep sound. "I can't wait to tell Jared you called him a goon."

"Like he can do anything about it."

"True, very true. See, I knew you liked being my fiancé."

"Why do you keep calling me that?" I looked over my shoulder, hoping there weren't too many people listening.

"Would you rather I call you my mate? Or is it wife you want? I thought fiancé sounded more normal for a college freshman."

"Because so many college freshman are engaged?" I tapped my pen, taking out my frustration on an inanimate object. "Why do you need to call it anything?"

"Do you have a better explanation for the ring on your finger?"

"Please. Girls wear rings on their left ring finger. I can explain it another way." I couldn't resist another peek at the ring. It was beautiful. If it weren't for the fact that it symbolized the end of my life as I knew it, I might have enjoyed wearing it.

"But it's not just any ring. It's my ring, and plenty of people know that. Don't forget it." His expression darkened, his light teasing replaced by something far more serious.

"So you really expect me to pretend we're engaged?"

"We don't have to pretend. Whenever you get tired of that dorm room, there's plenty of room in my bed."

"This is temporary, Levi. Temporary." I looked down, unable to meet his eye.

"I know, years from now we'll look back and laugh at the games you played."

"That's not what I meant, and you know it."

"Please, Al. I was part of that kiss."

I forced myself to meet his eye. "And it was just a kiss."

"It could have been more." He leaned over, whispering in my ear, "So much more."

"Cut that out, or I'm changing seats."

"We can talk about this more later."

"Later?"

"Yeah, there's an event at Commander's tonight you need to be at."

"Commander's? As in the restaurant?"

"What else would I mean?"

"What kind of event is it?" I wouldn't have admitted it, but he had my interest.

"A meeting." I noticed he didn't have either a notebook or laptop ready to take notes.

"A meeting? You're not going to give me more than that?"

"A meeting you need to be at." He gave me his usual cocky grin before turning toward the front of the room just as the professor walked in.

Class was uneventful, other than the professor telling us we had to form small groups for some semester long project.

"I think we'll make a great group." Levi took my books before I could stop him.

"Please, we are not working together. And I need my books back."

"I'm just carrying them for you. You'll get them back at your dorm."

"But we're practically there already." Like French, Art History was right next to my dorm.

"So, it's really not a big deal."

"Fine," I sighed. It was impossible to shake him off.

"I'll be over to get you at seven."

"Hailey and I can just take a cab." One of the annoying parts of being a freshman is that we couldn't have our cars on campus.

"What are you talking about? Hailey isn't coming."

I grabbed his arm. "Yes, she is. I'm not going without her."

"Are you serious? Do you realize how ridiculous that is?"

"What's ridiculous is you expecting me to go to a meeting with you with zero advance warning. What if I had plans?" I released his arm, backing away.

"Plans? You don't have plans."

"It's a Thursday night. Everyone goes out on Thursdays. We were going to check out Margarita Night at Vera Cruz."

"If we get out early, I'll take you." He put a hand on the back of his neck. "Besides, I can get you cheap Margaritas anytime."

"That's not the point of going, and you know it. Anyway, I'm not budging. You want me to come, Hailey's in too." I put a hand on my hip.

"Fine. But I'm driving you both. There is no way we're showing up separately."

"Deal. See you at seven."

"It's a date."

"No, it's a meeting."

He ran a hand down my arm, giving me goose bumps. "Remember what I said, one day we'll be laughing about this."

"Keep telling yourself that." I pulled my books from him and prepared to walk away.

"Oh, and try to wear something red tonight. If it happens to be short, I won't mind either."

I glared at him. "What's with you and red?"

"It's a family color."

"See you later, Levi."

***

Hailey was highlighting in her anthropology book when I got back to our room. "Hey, how was class?"

"Levi was in it."

She laughed. "So, in other words, it was fantastic."

"I think I'd use another word." I dropped my books on my desk, leaving my tote bag on my desk chair.

"Yeah, I bet."

"But, he did tell me about some meeting at Commander's Palace. He's picking us up at seven." I kicked off my flip flops.

"What? Did you just say *us*?" Hailey set her book down.

"Yeah. I refused to go without you."

"Oh my god, I love you, Allie Davis." She threw her highlighter across the room when she got up to hug me.

I laughed, detangling myself from her embrace. "I take it you wanted an invite?"

"This is huge. I never get invited to meetings, let alone one this big. Owen didn't even get to go until last year. Wow. I can't believe it."

"Owen didn't go until last year? Why? Was that Levi's first?"

"No, Levi's been going for years, and so has Jared. They didn't invite Owen until he was twenty-one and only because Levi insisted on it."

"So why did Jared get to go?" I kind of assumed Owen and Jared were pretty much equals.

"Jared gets to go because of his dad. Do you know anything about Jett Florence?"

"That's Jared's dad, I take it. I have no idea who he is." I sat down on my bed, leaning my back against the wall.

"I guess you could call him our General. He runs all

security and military for The Society."

"Oh. So where do you and Owen fit in?"

Hailey picked up her highlighter from the floor. "My dad's an engineer. He doesn't have an official position with The Society. You can't repeat this, but they're banking on Levi giving Owen a spot so our family gets more clout."

"So they must like that we're friends and everything." I had no clue where Hailey and her family fit in the hierarchy. I'd always assumed they were high up.

"Definitely. I think they're just scared I'm going to do something to screw things up. I did send you running into the arms of the Cougars."

"You did not! That was all Levi. Don't let anyone blame you."

"I just couldn't lie to my friend, even if it was to help Levi." She sat back down on her bed.

"Can I ask you something?"

"Sure." Hailey looked nervous.

"I think I already know the answer, but I need to hear it from you. You're not just my friend and roommate because it's a job, right?"

"No way! I liked you way before any of that. It just works out that I can protect you at the same time, you know?"

"Yeah, it does."

"So, now can we talk about fun things?"

I laughed. "Fun things?"

"What are we wearing tonight?"

"Levi wants me to wear red."

She picked up a skirt she had lying out on her bed. "Of course, he does."

"What's all of that about? He just said it's his family color. It has to do with all the ruby stuff, right?"

"Yeah. The ruling family chooses a stone to represent them."

The pieces started fitting together. "Oh...so my wearing red, like I did at the party at his house this summer, shows that I'm one of them."

"Yes. But I think Levi also just thinks you look hot in red."

"He also asked me to wear something short, so you're probably not too far off."

"Are you in the mood to torture him?"

"Torture him?"

Hailey went over to her closet and pulled out a short, red, halter dress.

"Are you serious?"

"It's going to look incredible on you, and technically you're doing what he asked. It's red and short, but it's also going to drive him mad. It'll probably remind him who really has the power."

"Does the fact that I'm totally going to do it make me evil?"

"No, it makes you normal. You're mad at him, but you also want him—a sexy dress serves both purposes."

I threw a pillow at her. She ducked out of the way. "What? Are you going to deny either of those charges?"

I wanted to deny the second one, but I couldn't. "We kissed." I buried my face in my hands.

"You kissed? When? Was it on move in day? It was, wasn't it?"

"Yes."

"What kind of kiss?" She sat forward.

"The 'it almost became much more' kind."

"Yeah, you really want him."

"I know." I turned and flopped back on my bed.

"You do realize that it isn't a bad thing, right? It makes things easier, and it isn't something to feel bad about."

"Is this friend Hailey speaking, or Pteron Hailey?"

"Both." She came to sit on the edge of my bed. "Are you going to tell me about the kiss?"

"It was just a really good kiss."

"As good as before…"

"Yeah, if not better because I missed kissing him. Oh

my god, what's wrong with me, Hailey? I can't feel this way after what he did to me."

"Why not? I'm not telling you to go jump him or anything, but you can't just ignore the feelings either—why not have some fun? Wear the dress."

"Only if you wear something sexy too. I'm not going to be the only one."

"Deal. There are a few boys going I wouldn't mind catching the eyes of."

"You could probably attract them in pajamas."

"Just like you could turn on Levi, but if you're doing it, you might as well do it in style."

"All right, let's do this."

CHAPTER FIVE

I checked my reflection in the mirror one more time before grabbing a black clutch and following Hailey out of the room. I'd opted to go with some stilettos, and I hoped my feet wouldn't hate me by the end of the night.

If someone's jaw could actually be on the floor, Levi's would have been when we walked outside. He was waiting for us impatiently. His face was set in a frown until he noticed us approaching. The frown quickly became something else entirely.

"Wow, you look incredible." He took a few steps closer to me.

"Thanks." I turned around to give him the full effect. "Does it meet your specifications?"

"Do I need to answer that?"

"What about me? Do I look incredible?" Hailey teased.

"Of course, Hailey. Although you're not old enough to wear a dress like that."

"I'm the same age as Allie." She glared at him.

"You'll always be twelve to me."

Hailey shook her head. "You're worse than Owen."

Levi shrugged. "I'm just being honest. Shall we?" He

gestured toward where he parked his black BMW over on the street.

"Sure." I linked arms with Hailey before he could even try to put an arm around me.

Levi opened up both the passenger door and the backdoor behind it.

I moved toward the back. "You can sit in the front, Hail."

"No, I don't mind the back."

I didn't miss the look that passed between them.

I took a seat, and Levi lingered for a moment before closing my door.

"I don't have to remind you how important it is that you go along with everything tonight, do I?" He pulled out onto the road.

"No, I get it." I looked out the window, annoyed at myself for how much I liked the way he looked in the navy sports coat he was wearing. I distracted myself by watching how the moonlight lit up the beautiful live oak trees. There really was something almost magical about New Orleans.

He put a hand on my bare leg. "Al?"

"Yeah?" I looked toward him.

"You really do look incredible."

"You don't look so bad yourself." I heard Hailey laugh and turned around to see her making a kissing face. She was lucky I couldn't reach her.

Levi laughed. He must have seen her in the rearview mirror.

"So, is there anything I should know before we get there?" If I was going into the lion's den, I wanted to be prepared.

"Nothing other than the fact that my dad thinks you agreed to marry me next summer."

I reached up and grabbed the 'oh my god' bar. "Excuse me?"

"Chill out, we can always tell him we pushed it off further, but he was worried. If I didn't say that, he would have called your dad to make sure he wasn't the problem. I figured you preferred it this way."

I sighed. "It is preferable to getting my dad involved. It was bad enough telling him I wasn't going to Princeton."

"I told you I'd talk to him…"

"And what would that have helped?"

"He likes me—or at least he likes my name." That was the first time Levi had acknowledged my dad's response to his background and money.

"Please tell me the wedding is the only surprise."

"It is. You might get a few questions about why you aren't living with me. Obviously, the wedding is just a formality for you and the outside world."

"I'll just say I'm traditional."

Hailey laughed again. "You obviously realize they know you two have slept together, right? I mean you wouldn't be his mate otherwise."

"Yeah, but that doesn't mean I'd want to move in with him." I looked at Levi even though I was answering Hailey.

Levi turned, and I knew we were getting close. I took a deep breath; I could handle this. Levi squeezed my leg, and I realized he hadn't moved his hand the whole drive. I hadn't stopped him. Levi grinned as he watched my realization. I groaned.

Levi stopped the car, and a guy came around immediately to open his door. There was something funny about him, but I couldn't place it. He was large and bulky. "Hello, Sir. Welcome."

Levi nodded, leaving his keys and coming around the car to open the door for both of us. He helped me out and put an arm around my waist. I didn't shake it off. I needed to play the part. Even Hailey had reiterated about twenty times how important this meeting was.

"That valet wasn't human, was he?" I asked quietly before we reached the entrance.

He leaned in. "Nope. He's a Silver."

"Oh, but he wasn't silver."

Levi laughed lightly. "Silver as in silverbacks."

"A gorilla?" I gasped.

"Exactly."

I nodded. I guess I'd eventually get used to all of these new groups. Well, only if I stuck around long enough to find out.

"You ready?"

"As ready as I'll ever be." I glanced behind me to make sure Hailey was with us. She was grinning. At least I was able to get her into this meeting—one positive thing.

I looked up at the large, blue and white restaurant. Even before I had visited New Orleans, I'd heard of Commander's Palace.

"Allison, it's lovely to see you again." Levi's dad came over and shook my hand—the one that wasn't currently pressed against Levi's side. I wasn't about to correct the king of a supernatural society on the use of my full name, even if he did ask me to call him Dad.

I gave him the brightest smile I could muster. "Hi Robert. It's great to see you."

"Hello, Hailey," he greeted her politely.

It took Hailey a moment to respond. "Mr. Laurent, thank you for having me tonight."

"Of course. I hope you enjoy the evening. If you ladies don't mind, I need to borrow my son. I think Helen's already inside if you want to go find her."

"Great, I look forward to seeing her."

"See you in a few minutes," Levi whispered before kissing me lightly.

"Don't take too long," I said flirtatiously. If I was playing the part, I was going to have fun with it.

Hailey and I walked further inside but before we could get too far, a tall guy stopped us. He blatantly checked me out before his eyes settled on my face and he grinned. He reached for my hand. "Bryant Florence. I'm sure I haven't had the pleasure of meeting you before, because there is no way I'd forget you." He shook my hand, holding it for longer than socially appropriate.

I stole a glance at Hailey. "Florence? So you're related to Jared?"

"You know my brother?" He watched me, like he was trying to reevaluate me.

"Yeah, I know your brother."

"It's unfortunate you met him first. I assure you he doesn't represent the family."

I felt a surprising offense at the way he talked about Jared, almost protective.

Hailey jumped in before I could say anything. "Bryant, do you know who this is?"

"No, I'm still waiting for her to give me her name."

"Her name's Allie. Allie Davis."

A look of shock crossed his face. "Oh shit. I'm sorry, I had no idea—"

"No harm done." I took a step back.

"Tell that to Levi," Hailey mumbled.

She took my hand and led us away. "He's worse than Jared. He's been in Paris for a few years. I have no idea why he's back."

I looked over my shoulder, and he was still watching me.

I saw Helen, Levi's mom, and decided we should head over. I glanced at Hailey and she nodded.

"Hi, Helen."

She turned, pausing in her conversation. "Allie." She immediately pulled me into a hug. "How are you doing? How have your first few days been?"

"Pretty good. I have an awesome roommate." I smiled at Hailey.

"I bet. It's wonderful you girls are so close. I'm sure it's made the transition easier. And Hailey, we're so glad you were able to make it tonight. Have you talked to your parents today? I invited them as well."

"My parents? They're here?"

"They should be."

"Well that was really generous." Hailey was already looking around the room.

"We really do appreciate everything you and your brother have done to help the family."

Hailey beamed, her attention returning to Helen. Sometimes I forgot how important The Society was to Hailey, but it was obviously huge.

One of the women Helen had been talking to moved to join us. She edged Hailey out of the way in the process. "Hi, Allie. I didn't get a chance to meet you at your party. I'm Missy, and it's an honor to meet you."

An honor? This was all so weird. I just smiled awkwardly. "It's nice to meet you too."

"You know, I have a daughter just a few years older than you. She's at Tulane, too. Let me give you her number so you girls can meet up and get coffee or something."

Annoyed at the way she treated Hailey, I cut her off. "That sounds nice, but I'm just getting settled. Hopefully, I'll meet her sometime soon."

I nervously looked toward Helen, hoping I hadn't just committed some huge social faux pas, but she smiled. I really loved Levi's mom.

We told Helen we'd talk more later, and headed over to grab something to drink. "Thanks," Hailey said as soon as we were out of earshot.

I took a sip of my champagne. "That was obnoxious."

"Yeah, her daughter's worse. There aren't many girls our age, and she always treated me like garbage."

"I definitely don't need to meet her then."

"You rock." Hailey smiled.

"So do you."

"Hello ladies." Jared sauntered over.

I waved with my free hand. Any familiar face was welcome that night. "Hey. I just met your brother."

"Yeah? Did he talk your ear off?"

"No, he tried to pick Allie up." Hailey took a sip from her glass.

"No way." Jared laughed. "Is she being serious?" He turned toward me.

"Yeah. It was pretty awkward." I didn't mention the way Bryant had talked about him.

"I'll have to remember that the next time he goes off on me. Dad would kill him for that."

"In his defense, he didn't know."

Jared reached over me to grab a glass for himself. "He should have figured it out. He's supposed to be so incredible at security. He should at least know what our princess looks like."

"Oh, there are my parents." I followed Hailey's gaze across the room and saw an attractive, middle aged couple. "Do you want to meet them?"

"Sure, that would be nice."

I said goodbye to Jared and followed Hailey over to them. "Hey guys, this is Allie."

"Allie, hello. It's wonderful to meet you finally." Hailey's mom smiled warmly and shook my hand.

"It's nice to finally meet you, too."

Her dad shook my hand as well. "It really is a pleasure."

I didn't miss the way they beamed at Hailey and how happy she looked.

"It's just been so nice to have Hailey around. It's only been a few days, but she's the best roommate."

"We're glad to hear that. She hasn't had to share a room before, but I'm sure she'll be a very thoughtful roommate."

"I'm not too worried. As long as she keeps her mess to her side, we're fine."

"Mess? Hailey—" The mortification on her mother's face had me jumping in immediately.

"I'm joking."

"Oh, good." Her mom's shoulders relaxed. "Oh wait,

we never introduced ourselves. I'm Jan and this is Timothy."

"Great, it's nice to have names other than Hailey's mom and dad."

It could have gotten awkward, but Owen joined us.

"Hey."

"Hey." I smiled. I hadn't seen Owen since French.

"Levi was looking for you, Allie."

"Oh? Where is he?" I started scanning the room.

"He was heading toward the dining room when I saw him."

"I should find him. I'll catch up with you in a few, Hailey."

I felt my phone vibrating but didn't want to check to see who it was in the middle of the room. I turned down a corridor. It was a text from Jess checking in. I'd have to call back. It had taken weeks for things to feel normal between us again after she left New Orleans suddenly. Even though she told me not to, I still blamed Jared for making her leave. Maybe it was for the best in the end though. She was head over heels for Emmett, and from what I knew, she was loving NYU.

I was about to look for Levi again when I heard a few voices. "You better not screw anything up. I know you're Levi's favorite pet but if you upset his girl, you're going to be in a world of trouble." I peeked over and saw Jared and Bryant talking to an older man who shared their black hair. I assumed he was their father, Jett. Had he seriously called Jared Levi's pet?

"You should talk? You—" Jared started.

Jett Florence spoke and it gave me chills. "You can't rely on Levi's friendship. He can change his mind and pick someone else. Don't screw this up, as usual, for the family."

I quietly slipped back out into the room. I noticed Levi talking to a man and went right over. I put a hand on his arm to get his attention.

He wrapped his arm around my waist. "Hey, sweetie, I was just looking for you."

"Owen told me."

"Allie, I don't believe you've met Mark yet. He's one of Dad's advisors."

"It's nice to meet you."

"The pleasure is mine." He shook my hand.

"You ready to find our seats?" Levi asked.

"Sure."

He led us into the dining room we were using.

Unsurprisingly, Levi was seated at the head of one of the tables. He pulled out the chair directly next to his, and I took a seat. Robert was already seated at the other end with Helen at his side. I watched as others filed in, taking seats around us.

I leaned over to whisper in Levi's ear. "We eat before the meeting?"

"Yes. We used to do it the other way around, but somehow it goes smoother when people are already fed."

I laughed. "I think that's the case with most things."

"Hello again, Allie." I turned away from Levi and saw Bryant sitting next to me.

"Hi."

I heard laughter and looked across from me in time to catch Jared's eye. Owen was seated next to him with Hailey a few seats further down. I wished Hailey were sitting closer to me, but I assumed it was a hierarchy thing.

"Is something funny, Jared?" Bryant said snidely.

I really didn't like Bryant.

A waiter came over and poured me a glass of red wine. I noticed no one was drinking it, so I waited for the toast that had to be coming.

Robert stood up. "Welcome to the Autumn meeting. It's nice to see you all here tonight. We have a lot to discuss, but first let us enjoy our meal."

He sat down and immediately a bowl of soup was placed in front of me. It smelled good, but I had no idea what it was.

"It's turtle soup," Levi explained.

"Turtle? Oh." It smelled good, but it was definitely a first for me.

"It's good, trust me."

I nodded. Levi definitely had good taste when it came to food.

I took a small spoonful, and Levi was right. It was fantastic.

"Like it?" he asked.

"Yeah." The soup was rich and warm.

"Good."

I knew that proper dinner party etiquette demanded I talk to Bryant, but I resisted until he spoke to me again. "What do you think of college so far? Is it what you expected?"

"It's been interesting."

"A good interesting?"

"Mostly." I savored the final spoonful of the soup.

"I heard you are living on campus. I'm sure Levi doesn't like that." He moved, and his leg brushed against mine. I scooted over in my seat just a little.

Was he seriously talking about this with Levi sitting next to me?

"I'm sure a few more nights of dorm life will have you moving in with him. It makes more sense that way."

He had to know that Levi could hear, so he must have thought this would somehow make him look good in Levi's eyes.

"I'm happy on campus. I miss Levi, but it's important to me. Luckily, Levi is really understanding and doesn't mind." I turned toward Levi with a smile.

"I never said I didn't mind. But as long as you keep spending nights with me, I'm fine with it until the wedding."

I swallowed down the response I wanted to give, and played along. "You know I'll keep spending nights with you. How could I resist?"

I felt Levi put a hand on my leg. "I'm just glad I get to take you home tonight." His hand slid up my leg, right below my thigh.

"I can't wait." I looked across the table and was met with Jared's smirk.

I was saved from more embarrassing conversation, or Levi's hand doing anything else, when our steak arrived. Thankfully, Levi needed both hands to cut it.

I glanced at Hailey. She looked at me sympathetically.

I finished my first glass of wine but declined a refill. With all of Levi's talk, I couldn't afford to get drunk around him.

I thought I was too stuffed to eat anything else until dessert came out. I jumped a little in surprise when the waiter set it on fire.

Levi touched my hand to get my attention. "Bananas foster."

I turned back to the cart with the dessert. "Nice presentation."

It was delicious—bananas, caramel and vanilla ice cream. I literally ate every bite.

"I see you like things sweet," Bryant said, barely audible above the voices around us. I looked over and he had a hungry look in his eyes, and it wasn't for more dessert. I turned toward Levi, but he hadn't heard. Was he seriously hitting on me again?

I could feel Bryant's eyes still on me. "I like dessert, yes. What girl doesn't?"

I didn't wait for his response. I scooted closer to Levi. Levi felt me shift. "Is everything okay?"

Either I was showing my emotions more than I thought, or Levi really knew me. I hoped it was the first. "Everything's fine."

"You sure?"

"Yeah." I certainly wasn't going to cause a scene at the party. I'd try to keep my distance from Bryant though.

After dessert was cleared away, Levi touched my arm. "You ready?"

"Where do we go for the meeting?"

"You can't guess?"

"Wait, is it at the hotel?"

"Of course." He took my hand. Hailey was talking to the guy next to her, who I recognized as the bouncer from Bruno's, but Levi interrupted. "You coming, Hailey?"

"I'll meet you there." She smiled, so I just waved.

I let Levi lead me out with a hand on my back. The valet pulled his car around as soon as he reached the front.

Levi opened my door for me, closing it before going around to his side.

"So what did you think of dinner?" He turned on the radio to some rock station, adjusting the volume to a barely audible level that made me wonder why he bothered with it at all.

"It was really good."

"Are you going to tell me what's wrong?"

"No."

He took his eyes off the road to look at me. "I love your honesty, Al, but I need to know."

"I'll tell you after the meeting." I knew he wouldn't give up, but I didn't want to rile him up before something important.

"Back at my place?" He smiled sheepishly.

"You do realize I'm not coming over, right?"

He let out a deep breath. "Unfortunately, I'm painfully aware. I figured that out when you stopped after one glass of wine."

"Very perceptive."

"I'm always perceptive when it comes to you."

Not always. He'd totally missed Bryant coming on to me.

He pulled up out front of the hotel in a spot that seemed to have been left open for him. I walked in, relieved that Billy, my friend who worked as a bell boy, wasn't there. I hadn't been back in a few weeks, but I'd spent the whole summer working at the hotel my dad owned. My friend, Alex, was working at the bar, and he just shook his head when he saw me walk in with Levi. I waved, pretending I didn't notice his disapproval.

We walked over to the elevators, and I followed Levi in. I waited as he pushed the button for the basement, inserting a key card that allowed us to go to a floor of the building that didn't officially exist. Knowing we were about to enter pitch blackness, I grabbed on to Levi's hand. He'd be able to see perfectly. Levi squeezed my hand as the doors opened, and we walked out into the blackness.

CHAPTER SIX

So much had changed since the last time I'd walked down the marble floored hallway of the basement. Now I knew Levi was a prince, and that I'd become some sort of princess. I was glad to have his large, strong hand wrapped around mine as we walked into the chambers. It made the entrance at least a little less intimidating.

Owen and Jared both stood up as we walked in. We'd barely taken two steps into the room when they met up with us.

Levi turned to me. "I have to sit with my dad, so you don't mind sitting with them, do you?"

I was okay as long as he wasn't leaving me alone. "No, it's fine. Hopefully Hailey will get here soon."

"Aw, missing me already, roomie?" Hailey joined us.

"I miss you every time we're apart."

"The feeling's mutual, babe. Completely mutual." She linked arms with mine, and I waved goodbye to Levi as we followed Jared and Owen over to a couple of stone seats that were part of a circular pattern with multiple levels of stadium seating.

The chamber was cold and the bare skin of my legs

against the cool stone wasn't ideal. "Next time, we're wearing pants."

Hailey laughed. "Agreed."

I looked around for Levi, but I couldn't find him. Jared leaned over to talk to me. "He's going to enter with his dad."

"So it's different from the ball then? Because shouldn't Allie be with him?" Hailey turned to Jared.

"It's completely different. This is business."

"Ball?" I asked.

"Yeah, there's an annual ball each winter."

"Oh."

"Trust me, you'll hear all about it. I'm sure Helen's already planning your dress." Hailey crossed her legs.

"My dress?"

"Of course."

I decided to ask the question on my mind even if I got made fun of for it. "Does Levi usually just bring random dates?"

Jared laughed. "You jealous, Allie?"

"No, just curious."

"He always went alone. It wouldn't have been appropriate for him to bring someone other than his mate," Hailey explained.

I tried to ignore the flood of relief I felt. "Oh, cool."

"Levi's going to love that you were jealous." Owen tried to stretch out his long legs. In addition to being cold, the stone seats were cramped.

I crossed my arms, half out of annoyance and half from the cold. "Come on, I was just curious."

Jared arched an eyebrow. "Keep telling yourself that."

"Whatever."

The room grew quiet and everyone stood up. I followed their lead, looking toward the doorway. A procession of men filed in. Then Levi came in, followed by his father. They took seats in the center of the room. As soon as they were seated, everyone else sat too. "Levi usually sits behind him," Jared whispered.

"What's changed?"

He pointed at me. "You."

"What's that supposed to mean?"

"Taking you as his mate let his dad know he was ready. He's letting him transition into leadership. Levi is now his senior advisor. He'll eventually take over, of course."

"Levi never told me that."

Jared leaned back in his seat. "Not surprising."

Levi looked over to where we sat and smiled at me. I smiled back. I had to admit there was something cool about being with someone in such a respected position.

I jumped as I heard a loud bang. "It's just the doors closing and locking," Jared explained.

"Locking?"

"No one's allowed in or out until the proceedings are completely over."

I shivered. The chilly temperature of the room was only accentuated by the fact that I was locked in a room with paranormal creatures. The thought scared me more than a little. I wrapped my arms tighter around myself.

Levi glanced at me and got up. "What's he doing?" I said to myself as he walked directly over to me.

Stopping right in front of us, he took off his blazer and put it over my shoulders. "This should help." He kissed me on the cheek before taking his seat. His father gave him an approving smile. I wondered if the chivalrous display was really about helping me, or if it was for appearances sake.

"Welcome all." Robert stood and addressed the room. "The Autumn meeting is officially in session. We will follow the usual schedule tonight. Before I turn the floor over to my advisors, I want to emphasize the importance of discretion. Nothing discussed tonight may leave the room." He continued to describe the rules and introduced his advisors. Listening to Robert, I could have been in a trance. He definitely had the gift of public speaking.

Each advisor took turns making presentations, but none really caught my attention until Jett Florence stood. I knew he was head of security, but I didn't realize he was also an advisor. It seemed to be setup kind of like a president and his cabinet.

"The threat of the Blackwell's has grown. We have reason to believe they're planning to take out the Laurent line from within."

A few gasps filled the room. "We will, of course, determine the reliability of this intelligence, but until then, I urge all of you to use caution. If you have any suspicions, you need to report them to my department immediately.

That brings me to my next point, the need to increase the security force. I want to take on an additional officer within the next year."

Robert interrupted. "I assume Jared will be taking that position."

I looked over at Jared, his face was emotionless.

Jett cleared his throat. "I am not sure he's ready for the job."

"How can you say that?" Levi lashed out. I had to admire his loyalty to his friend.

Jett's expression didn't waver, even when Levi directed his anger at him. "Bryant and I aren't sure he's prepared."

"What?" I hadn't realized I'd spoken out loud until I felt Hailey's hand on my arm.

"Do you have something you'd like to say, Allison?" Robert asked.

I don't know what came over me, but I remembered how rude Jared's brother and dad had been earlier. Bryant was coming on to Levi's mate, and Jared wasn't ready?

"Yes, I have something to say." I slipped my arms through the sleeves of Levi's coat.

"What are you doing?" Hailey whispered.

Robert looked amused. "You have my permission to address the assembly."

I swallowed and stood up. "How can you say that Jared

isn't ready?"

"Is there a reason you think my judgment is unsound?" Jett asked, his face a mask of stone.

The whole room had turned to look at me, but no one said a word.

"Jared saved my life. Doesn't saving the life of your prince's mate count for something?"

I didn't realize it until after the words were out, but that was the first time I'd admitted I was Levi's mate.

Robert chuckled. "Yes, it does. So I take it you support Jared's installment as a security officer after his graduation?"

"Yes. It's no secret Jared and I haven't always seen eye to eye." There were some laughs. "But I wouldn't hesitate to trust him completely."

Robert nodded. "Thank you for sharing your opinion. It will be taken into consideration."

"Thank you." I pulled Levi's jacket tighter around myself and sat down. I risked a glance over at Levi, and he was grinning at me. Evidently, he approved.

"Who are you, and what did you do with my best friend?" Hailey whispered loudly.

I just shrugged.

Jared leaned over. "I have no idea where that came from, but thanks. I owe you."

"I'll remember that."

Jared made so much more sense to me. His arrogance was at least somewhat explained by his jerk of a brother, and anyone whose dad could publicly degrade him like that deserved some understanding in my book. I wondered what Jett would think if he knew about the way Bryant had treated me.

I tried to pay attention to the rest of the proceedings, but I was still dealing with the post adrenaline rush from having spoken against a man like Jett Florence. I had a feeling I was one of the first.

The night wore on, and it had to have been at least

three o'clock by the time Robert closed the meeting. The doors finally opened.

"Want to just stay upstairs and take the streetcar to class?" I asked Hailey.

"Oh yeah, you still have your room." Hailey nodded enthusiastically. "That sounds great."

I stood up with everyone else as Levi and his father left.

"Levi will probably be a bit, but we can wait for him upstairs," Owen offered.

"Can you just tell him Hailey and I are staying in my room here? I'm too tired to go anywhere."

"Sure, want us to go up with you?" Jared was looking at me differently. He was probably trying to figure out why in the world I defended him.

"I think we'll make it." I moved out of the way as people maneuvered around us to reach the exit.

"All right, sleep well." Jared looked relieved that he didn't have to worry about me. I'm sure he was exhausted too.

"We will." Hailey linked arms with me again, and I let her lead us to the elevator. Her super vision came in handy.

Once back in my room, I gave Hailey some extra clothes, and changed into a t-shirt. I was glad I'd left a few things in my dresser. We barely said anything before we both collapsed.

I woke up groggily when I heard a noise coming from the main sitting area. I doubted Hailey had left the other bedroom in the suite so I got up to check.

I wasn't surprised when I saw Levi standing by the open balcony door. He was shirtless, and his wings were still extended. He must have just landed. He retracted his large, black wings.

"Don't you knock?"

He grinned. "I didn't want to wake you up."

"So what was your plan?"

"Ideally, I was going to sneak into your bed, but I guess I was louder than I thought."

"No, I just don't sleep deeply anymore." We both knew why that was. Getting kidnapped by cougar shifters and almost raped can do that to a girl.

I looked away. Seeing him without a shirt was doing a number on me.

He noticed. "Still going to tell me you don't want to work things out?"

"Yes, but I'm too tired to argue."

"I just wanted to tell you that you were awesome tonight. Plus, you did promise to tell me what upset you."

I'd hoped he'd forgotten. "Okay, but we need to be quiet. I don't want to wake up Hailey."

"I can do quiet."

I sat down on the couch next to him, not even caring that I was only wearing a t-shirt. He'd seen me in less. "I don't want you going off your handle."

"I can't promise that. If someone did something to upset you, there will be consequences."

I already saw his eyes changing. I couldn't set him off. It wasn't worth it.

"It really wasn't anything. I—I just kind of wished we didn't have to pretend." It wasn't a lie. It had gone through my head more than once. I wished Levi hadn't hurt me so bad that I could never trust him again.

A slow smile spread across his face. "Why would I get mad about that?" His eyes went from black to heated. "I don't want to pretend either."

"You'd be mad that it still doesn't change things."

"It will one day. It has to." He scooted closer to me. "We belong together." His breath was warm on my face and he put an arm around me. "I've missed you so much."

"I've missed you too, but it doesn't matter." I closed my eyes. It was so late, and I couldn't fight the exhaustion anymore. I felt Levi shift us so that we were lying down, his arms wrapped around me.

I forced words out even as I felt myself drift toward sleep. "I shouldn't fall asleep with you."

"You've slept with me on the couch before. I'll be good."

"I know." I was vaguely aware of him pulling the blanket off the back of the couch and covering us with it.

"Goodnight, Al."

"Night." I already knew it would be the best few hours of sleep I'd had in weeks.

***

"Morning, love," Levi said softly. I turned to look at him. It wasn't easy considering the size of Levi and the couch.

"Hi." One of Levi's hands was still wrapped around my waist—under my t-shirt. He didn't seem interested in moving it.

"Next time, let's use a bed. If I recall correctly, you have a perfectly good king size one in there."

I felt warm just thinking about how he knew that. That night had been incredible—the best night of my life. Too bad what happened afterwards was a nightmare.

"Thinking about it again, aren't you?" He used his free hand to brush some hair off my face. Strangely enough, I let him.

"Again?"

"You said my name a few times last night." He grinned.

"And that somehow meant I was thinking about that night."

"It's how you said it. The first time I answered, but then I realized you were sleeping. The next few times made it pretty obvious what you were dreaming about."

"I wasn't having sex dreams about you, Levi." I sat up, then stood as soon as I woke up enough.

Levi sat up and stretched. "Seriously, my back is killing me."

54

"It's not my fault. Whose idea was it to stay here?"

"I'm not saying it wasn't worth it. It was definitely worth it." He raked his eyes over me, and I suddenly felt self-conscious.

Hailey's door opened. "Well, hello there. What did I miss after I went to bed last night?"

"Good morning, Hailey." Levi got up to pull on the t-shirt he'd carelessly thrown over a chair when he came in the night before.

"You have a nine o'clock, right?" she asked.

"What time is it?"

"Eight twenty. If we get a cab, you'll make it back just in time to grab your books."

"I'll drive you," Levi offered.

"Normally I'd say no thanks, but I can't be late." I sighed with relief. Catching a cab in the morning could take a while.

"You're cute." Levi put a hand on the back of the couch.

"Excuse me?"

"You're honestly worried about being late to your econ class, aren't you?" He slipped into his black shoes.

"Of course, it's only the second day." I ignored the fact that he knew what class I had. That was old news.

"I just need to get dressed. Come with me Hailey, I'm sure you can find something too." She followed me, wearing the PJ pants and t-shirt I'd given her. I'd let her have the only pair of PJ pants. I wouldn't have if I'd known about the company.

Fifteen minutes later, we were slipping into Levi's car. "Thanks for the hospitality, Al. That was the best night's sleep I've had in a while."

It was mine too, but I kept the fact that I was still having nightmares to myself. "Glad to hear it, but don't expect it to happen again."

He started the engine. "It will. Very soon."

"No, it won't."

Hailey laughed. "You guys act like an old, married couple sometimes—wait you are mar—"

"Don't say it, Hail." I turned back to glare at her.

Levi put a hand on my leg. "Don't say married? See, telling everyone at school we're engaged isn't so bad, is it?"

I pushed his hand off even though I liked it there. I needed to put my resistance back up. I was getting dangerously close to giving in to him. Truthfully, I'd already given in. Letting him spend the night on the couch was a huge step in the wrong direction.

"So what are the plans this weekend?" he asked.

"I'd like to do something with some of the girls on our floor—we obviously never caught up with them last night."

"Same, we'll have to talk to Anne and Tiffany," Hailey agreed.

"Tonight?" Levi glanced into the rearview mirror.

"I guess."

"Okay, so let's hang out tomorrow night."

I shook my head. "I can't."

"Come on, Al. You know you want to. It doesn't even have to be just the two of us. We can hang out as a group."

I looked back at Hailey, and she shrugged.

I sighed, realizing this was another dangerous step. "I'll think about it."

He put a hand on the back of my seat. "I'll take it."

Levi turned on to Broadway and parked near our dorm. "I'll call you later to finalize plans."

"You never give up, do you?"

"Not when it comes to you."

Before I could unbuckle my seatbelt, he leaned over and did it himself, his lips brushing against mine. "Have a great day."

"See ya." I got out without looking back.

We went inside, and I grabbed my books before running across campus to make my first class.

I walked in after the professor had already started his lecture. He shot me an annoyed look as I slid into my seat next to Jared. Jared smiled at me, tilting his laptop so I could see his notes. Unlike Levi, Jared actually took them.

Class went by in a blur, and I walked out with Jared just like after our first class.

"Levi never came home last night. Do you know anything about that?"

I figured he'd find out anyway. "He may or may not have spent the night on the couch."

"And where did you sleep?"

"On the couch," I mumbled.

"You two sure like the couch. Is he going to be in a good mood when I see him?" Jared nudged me as we walked.

I moved closer to Jared when a kid on a bicycle nearly ran me over. "It depends on how happy cuddling makes him."

Jared arched a brow. "Cuddling. Is that what you kids are calling it these days?"

"You got me. We had hot sex. I wanted Hailey to join in, but Levi wasn't up for it."

Jared cracked up. "You're okay, Allie."

"I'm glad you approve."

"But seriously." He glanced behind us before continuing. "I'm glad you guys are working things out."

"I don't know if I'd say that..."

"You spent the night together. I don't care if all you did was sleep. It still means something. You don't do that with someone you don't want to be with."

I adjusted the straps of my tote bag so they didn't dig into the bare skin of my shoulder that my tank top left exposed. "I didn't want to be with him the last time we slept on the couch."

"Yes you did."

We reached my next class, and I saw Owen waiting in the same spot as last time.

Jared nodded. "See you around, Princess."

"Do you really have to do that?"

"What? It's your title."

I shook my head. Jared waved to Owen, and walked away.

"Good morning." Owen looked tired. I guessed he'd been up even later than I had.

"Before you ask, I spent the night with Levi on the couch."

He smiled. "I know."

"You do?"

"I just ran into him." Owen held open the door to our classroom.

"Oh, okay."

We headed into French class, and I hoped I'd manage to understand something my teacher said this time.

CHAPTER SEVEN

My first Friday night as a college student didn't start out particularly eventful.

"So, we'll go to the Boot first and see where we want to go from there." Anne applied her makeup in front of one of the mirrors in the bathroom.

"Didn't the guys say the Boot was lame?" I finished straightening my hair, unplugging the flat iron before placing it on the sink to cool.

"Upperclassman always say that. I think you burn out on it Freshman year because it's right here." The bar was literally a couple hundred feet from our dorm.

"Okay, I'm up for anything." I couldn't deny the giddiness I felt about going out with the girls. Even though it had only been three days of classes, I'd survived my first week of college.

I grabbed my purse and followed Anne out of the room. Hailey and Tiffany needed to use the ATM, so we were meeting up with them outside the bar.

The Boot was happening. People were hanging out on the sidewalk outside, and a steady stream was heading in. There was nothing particularly special about the place, but located right off campus, it was unofficially the Tulane bar.

We saw Hailey and Tiffany immediately, and wordlessly we all headed to the door.

We flashed our IDs at the bouncer and walked inside.

"One of the annoying parts about this place is that they actually check ID." Hailey replaced her license in her wallet.

"We can always get fakes if you think we need them." Anne definitely seemed keen on the idea.

Hailey shot her down. "We don't need them, and it's not worth the risk of getting busted with one."

"I never saw you as someone who would be afraid of getting caught," I said casually, taking in my surroundings. A bar dominated the back wall, with tables scattered throughout the rest of the space.

"I'm not, but it's not worth it when you can get served most places."

Tiffany nodded. "Yeah, that makes sense."

"I'm sure someone will get us beer." Anne smiled as Brandon came our way. I knew I wasn't imagining something between them at the frat party.

"Hey guys. We've got a table and a few pitchers, care to join us?"

We all looked at each other before Hailey answered. "Sure."

An hour and a few cups of beer later, Anne was agreeing on our behalf to go with the guys to some small house party their friend was throwing. Considering nothing too exciting was happening at the bar, none of us had a problem with it. It was really funny to be hanging out with Brandon. I never would have believed it in high school.

We walked a few blocks down Broadway with the guys, hoping the party would be at least half decent. We stopped in front of a house with faded paint and a rickety front porch. The only thing that marked it as a college student's house was the Tulane Green wave sticker on the front window.

I walked up the front steps, hoping they'd manage to hold all of our weight. This was one of those non-glamorous parts about college that people never tell you about—worrying that the dilapidated apartment hosting a party would fall apart with you in it.

There were only about twenty people inside when we arrived, so Tiffany, Hailey and I took a seat on a couch after grabbing some Abita beers. It didn't take much time in the city to realize it was a great local beer. Anne continued to chat with Brandon. There was definitely something going on between them.

A guy with shaggy, brown hair squeezed in next to me, pushing me closer to Hailey in the process.

"Hey, I'm Nick." He held out his hand, shifting his beer to his other hand.

"Hi, I'm Allie." I accepted the handshake. His hand was wet from what I hoped was condensation from his beer.

"Cool. I don't think I've seen you out before."

"Probably not. I'm a freshman."

"Really? I wouldn't have thought so."

"Because I look old?" I tried to discretely wipe my hand on my skirt.

"No, not at all." He looked panicked. "I just mean you seem more mature."

"Oh. I'm going to take that as a compliment."

He smiled. "You should."

There was something almost helplessly nerdy about Nick. He tried to hide it behind a frat boy front, but it was definitely there. I'd have felt bad for him if he wasn't blatantly violating my personal space. I scooted closer to Hailey, but I couldn't move far. The couch wasn't built for four.

"Hello, Hailey," a brunette said snidely. She was tall. Her long legs exposed in a short, black dress. A pair of three inch heels only added to the effect. No one had to tell me she was a Pteron. The confidence she carried screamed it.

"Hi, Michelle." Hailey almost flinched when she said her name.

"What are you doing here?" Michelle didn't even glance at me.

Hailey played with the clasp of her purse, obviously flustered. "We were invited."

"I didn't think these guys had such bad taste."

"Excuse me, who are you?" I asked. The girl was a brat.

She turned to study me, clearly not impressed by what she saw. "Was I talking to you?"

Hailey laughed. "Do you know who this is, Michelle?"

"Should I?"

"Allie, Allie Davis." Hailey grinned.

Michelle coughed, nearly choking on her beer. "You're Levi's Allie?"

I wouldn't normally want to admit to it, but I figured this had to be the daughter of the woman I'd met at Commander's. "Yes."

"Oh, wow, I didn't know." Her cheeks flushed.

I shrugged. "I don't usually go by Levi's Allie. Just Allie is fine."

She crossed her feet at her ankles in what I assumed was a nervous motion. "Can I get you something? A beer or anything?"

"I'm fine." I held up my half full beer in evidence. "You can stop trying to kiss up to me." I was still mad about the way she treated Hailey.

Tiffany looked between Michelle, Hailey, and I trying to figure it out. I was really glad it was Tiffany with us and not Anne. She didn't say anything.

Michelle's eyes suddenly lit up. "Does Levi know you're here?"

"He knows I'm out with my friends."

"He lets you go to parties without him?"

"Wow, you need to dump your boyfriend if he's that

controlling." Nick leaned closer to me.

Michelle broke into a smile. "He's more than her boyfriend."

"Okay… still you need to ditch him." Nick put a hand on my arm. I shrugged it off.

"It just surprises me he'd be okay with it. I'd have thought Levi would be more protective." Michelle leaned in like she was challenging me. Maybe being rude to her was a bad idea.

"I think I know Levi better than you do." I stood up. I didn't like having to look up at her. If it weren't for her higher heels, we would have been close to the same height. "Besides, he doesn't own me."

Her eyes darkened, but then she calmed down. "I guess you would know him better. It just seems odd that you'd be here flirting with other guys. I can't imagine Levi, or his father, would like that."

"His father?" Tiffany asked, talking for the first time.

"Yes, his father really wouldn't like it." I didn't like the way Michelle was looking at me. Warning bells went off. I couldn't let Robert find out the truth from Michelle. It was up to Levi to tell him.

"I'll be right back," I said to Hailey and Tiffany.

I walked out onto the front porch and texted Levi. I glanced up at the cross streets. *I'm at a party on Broadway and Maple. We planned to meet here. Come.*

I reclaimed my seat on the couch, knowing he'd be joining me soon.

Nick and Michelle were nowhere in sight, but I assumed neither had gone very far. "Everything okay?" Anne asked, abandoning Brandon.

"Everything's great." I smiled.

Hailey gave me a quizzical look before continuing to rip the label off her beer. She looked bored.

We sat for a while before I heard a very familiar voice. "Hey, I'm just looking for someone."

I turned and stood up. I saw Michelle out of the corner

of my eye as I launched myself into Levi's arms. "Finally!" As his arms came around me in surprise, I kissed him. He responded immediately, his arms tightening. I heard Jared and Owen laughing in the background.

I pulled away in a slight daze—it was supposed to be just for show, but it didn't feel that way.

"Hey, love, it's good to see you too." I could tell he was trying to figure out what was going on.

"I just met a friend of yours." I pointed to where Michelle stood with her arms crossed over her chest.

Understanding flashed in Levi's eyes as he led us over to her. "Hi, Michelle. So you've met Allie?"

Michelle moved her arms and stood up straighter. "Yes, and I definitely get why you chose her. She's amazing." She gave me the biggest, fakest smile.

The forced nature of it didn't go unnoticed by Levi. "Good. As nice as it is to see you, I'm going to be taking Allie now. We've got some plans of our own."

I groaned internally. I tried to help and, of course, he had to take advantage of it. "Before we go, let me make sure my friends don't mind."

"We don't mind at all," Anne said immediately. "Go have fun." She winked at me.

"If you want to go, we understand." Tiffany was trying to figure out what I wanted her to say.

"Yeah, go ahead." Hailey grinned. She was in so much trouble.

"Bye, Michelle. Great meeting you." I let Levi lead me to the front door.

"You guys staying?" Levi asked his friends.

"Yeah." Jared was eyeing Tiffany.

"Okay, but remember the rules," I warned him. Tiffany was too sweet of a girl to have to deal with Jared.

He glared at me. "Yes, how could I forget?"

Levi led us off the porch and away from the house.

"Nice kiss."

"You know why I did it." I looked up at the perfectly

crescent moon.

"Do I?"

He traced a line down my arm.

"Of course. Michelle would have told your dad if she thought something was up. Why would it mean anything else?"

"A chaste kiss could have accomplished the same thing. That wasn't chaste—your tongue was in my mouth, Al."

"Are you complaining?"

"Hell no. I happen to like your tongue...and the rest of you." His eyes let me know exactly what he was implying.

I stood staring at him for a moment. I wished he didn't make my whole body heat up a couple of degrees every time I was alone with him. "So, was making me leave part of fooling Michelle, or was there any other reason?"

"Of course, there were other reasons. Unlike you, I'm not pretending to want to stay away."

"Where'd you park?"

"I didn't drive."

"So you're walking me back to my dorm?" It wasn't too far, but I was regretting my decision to wear new shoes. My feet were killing me.

"Would you rather fly?" He smiled. "And be honest."

I probably should have said no, but a major part of me wanted to say yes and that part won over. "You'll fly me home?"

"You know I'd fly you anywhere."

"Fine."

He grinned, pulling off his shirt as he led us further into the shadows. He kissed my neck once before wrapping his arms around my waist and taking off from the sidewalk.

It had only been a few weeks since I'd last flown with Levi, but it felt like forever. The familiar exhilaration hit me as soon as we were airborne, and I wished my dorm was further away. Evidently, Levi did too.

"Where are we going?" I yelled. I knew he'd be able to

hear me over the wind, but I wouldn't hear his answer. When the city lights began fading from view, I had a pretty good idea. After a few minutes, he landed in the sand.

"What the hell, Levi? You were supposed to bring me home!"

"You didn't want to go home, did you?" He pulled me close to him, kissing my ear, before moving his lips back to my neck. I involuntarily closed my eyes.

"Did you?" he whispered.

Without conscious thought, I answered. "No."

"Good." He moved his lips to mine, but surprised me by giving me only the lightest of kisses. He took my hand and led me for a walk down the beach. "I've missed you so much."

"I've missed you too," I admitted. I looked out at the black water, wishing the moon were full like the last time we'd gone to Grand Isle.

"I knew you did." He grinned, pulling me down onto the sand with him.

"Nothing's changed, Levi. I'm still mad."

"Come on, things have changed. We spent last night together, and look at us now. Who do you think you're fooling?"

"I'm not just going to go back to how things were before. I can't."

"As long as the end result is the two of us together, and you coming home with me tonight, I'm okay with that."

"I'm not going home with you."

"Putting that part aside, can you at least admit we're together?" He leaned down over me, gently stroking my stomach under my tank top, in an all too familiar way.

"Only if we move things slow."

"Move things slow?" His hand stilled.

"We can date. But it's casual, and I am not sleeping with you."

"You slept with me last night."

I groaned. "Okay, I am not having sex with you."

"But you'll sleep in my bed?" His hand moved again, inching even further up my body.

"Not a chance."

"So, we're back to couches only? Good to know."

"I'm being serious. The last time we had sex, I ended up your mate. I'm not doing that again anytime soon."

"What, you think you'll become even more than a mate, or that if you let me have you too many times you'll be under my mind control?"

I froze.

"That's a joke, Al. I swear, no mind control."

"If my terms aren't acceptable, I can go back to avoiding you." We both knew I didn't really mean it.

"You can't avoid me, but I'll accept the terms for now."

"Good."

"So can I kiss you, or is that breaking some other term you randomly made up?" He shifted, his face inches above mine.

I smiled despite the fact that he was making fun of me. "You can kiss me."

I closed my eyes, waiting for his lips to meet mine again. He didn't disappoint. I would never get enough of his lips—or any part of him. I'd missed being with him, the way he set me on fire with the simplest touch.

His hand moved up more, resting on my breast. I moaned, knowing how good it would feel if his hand slipped under my bra. He surprised me by not trying it. Evidently, he did listen. We kissed for a few minutes more before he rolled away from me slightly, resting on his back. He took my hand, and we just stared up at the sky for a while. Eventually, my back protested from lying on the ground, and I stood up.

"Are you sure you don't want to go home with me?" Levi helped me brush sand off my skirt. His hands were wandering more than they needed to, and I knew before looking up just how heated a look he'd give me.

"Yes. I'm sure."

"Fine, but I know you're going to dream about me."

"You wish." I tried to shake the sand out of my hair.

"No. I know." He kissed me again before taking off toward home.

He landed right near my dorm. "I'll pick you up at nine o'clock tomorrow night."

"I never agreed."

"You will now. Hailey's invited too. I think it's time I showed you some more of my, uh, hangouts."

"Wait, a paranormal place?"

He nodded. "You in?"

"Definitely. I'll tell Hailey."

"Good night, Al." He kissed me gently.

"Night."

I walked inside knowing he was still watching. When I got back to my room, Hailey was waiting up.

"So do we still hate Levi, or is he back on the good list?" She stopped typing on her computer and turned toward me. She was already in her pajamas.

"We?"

"Yeah. We're on the same team."

I smiled. "He's not in the dog house anymore, but he's certainly not back in the bedroom."

"No, he's on the couch." She laughed.

"You're so funny."

"Come on, how perfect was that? But anyway, I'm glad. You look happy."

"I am. As angry as he makes me, he also makes me—"

"Hot?"

"That's one way of putting it." I slipped off my shoes, putting them back in the closet.

"Okay, he'll be back in the bedroom soon."

My phone beeped, signaling a text. *Sweet dreams.*

I texted back to Levi. *Wish you were here.*

I can be there.

It was a joke.

Not funny. Next time you do that expect to find me in your bed.

I didn't like the thrill that ran through me at the prospect. *I don't think Hailey would like that.*

I don't think I care.

Good night.

Night, Love.

"Are you done sexting with Levi?" Hailey smirked.

"Gross." I dug some pajamas out of my drawer.

"Stop pretending to be a prude, Allie, it's not fooling anyone."

"I love you, Hailey. You know that, right?"

"Of course, how could you not?"

I had no idea what was going to happen with Levi, but at least I had a friend along for the ride with me.

CHAPTER EIGHT

"Stay close to me tonight, Al." Levi held me tightly against his side as we walked away from where he parked his car on the dark street.

"This place is safe, right?" My excitement over seeing an actual paranormal bar subsided enough for me to realize I should probably be worried.

"It's perfectly safe if you stay with me." He squeezed my shoulder.

"It's too bad they won't think I'm a Pteron," I grumbled. It had been really cool when some Weres thought I was a Pteron. The only way you could tell someone was a Pteron was to wait for them to shift, and with my height, I'd managed to fool some guys. I liked everyone thinking I was that powerful.

"Sorry, Al. Everyone knows I wouldn't mate with anyone but a human."

"What if I have to go to the bathroom?"

"You'll go with me, of course." Hailey was a few steps behind us. I sensed she was protecting me too. I could make out Jared and Owen at the door.

The outside of the bar didn't look like much. Unlike

other bars, there were no neon signs, or other indications that the place was a public establishment. That was probably the point. If you didn't know about it, you shouldn't be there. The only hint that the place wasn't abandoned was the two large guys standing outside of it.

"Levi." The two bouncers said in unison as they bowed their heads slightly.

Levi never loosened his hold on me. I took comfort from being at his side.

There had to have been at least two hundred people in there—although I doubted many were people in the traditional sense. A large group congregated at the bar, while others sat at wooden tables. Levi headed right over to a table off in the corner. It felt distinctly like it was a table he frequented often. I felt all eyes on me as he pulled out my chair.

"I'll get us a couple rounds of shots." Jared didn't bother to sit down.

Levi sat next to me, and threw an arm over my shoulder. "I'd get you your favorite drink, but this isn't the kind of place for it."

"Oh," is all I said. I didn't like the way everyone was looking at me.

"You alright?" Levi carefully brushed some hair away from my face.

"Of course."

"You're not fooling me, but I'll pretend I believe you."

I smacked his arm playfully. "Don't forget you're still on probation."

"Probation? That's a new one. That could make for some interesting role play." His mischievous expression put me at ease. We might have been in a weird place, but he was still Levi.

"Levi—"

I was interrupted when Jared returned with a tray heaping with shots.

Levi handed one to me, before taking one for himself.

Hailey, Owen, and Jared each took a shot glass.

Levi held up his shot and everyone else followed. "To good times and the king."

I wasn't completely sure what the toast meant. I'd never head them toast Levi's dad before, but I took the shot. It burned on the way down. I doubted I'd ever be a shot person.

I'd waved away the second shot when I noticed a guy staring at me, literally licking his lips. He looked like he was in his mid-twenties, with reddish-brown hair. I nudged Levi to get his attention.

Levi growled. Jared, Owen, and Hailey turned around to see what he was looking at.

The man smiled, pushing back his chair and sauntering over.

"Hello, Levi."

Levi tensed beside me. "What do you want, Martin?"

"I just thought it would be appropriate to introduce myself to your mate."

"She doesn't want to meet you." Levi sat forward, attempting to block me from Martin's view.

"Oh, come on now, she looks friendly."

I stiffened, my leg pushing into Levi, wanting the comfort of his touch.

Martin never took his eyes off me. His expression was anything but friendly. It was like he was a predator examining his prey. It brought back some unwanted memories of the cougars.

Levi put a hand on my leg to calm me. "Go away, Martin."

"Is that anyway to treat your cousin?"

"Cousin?" I'd developed the awful habit of blurting out what was on my mind without thinking.

"Yes, hasn't Levi told you about me?" He tilted his head to the side in a way I'd only seen animals do.

"No…" I looked at Levi.

His face was blank.

"What a shame. I know a lot about you." He licked his lips again. "You're originally from New York, aren't you? I'm sure it was hard for you to leave."

I swallowed, determined not to let Martin see just how much he frightened me. "I miss it, but I like it here."

He smiled condescendingly. "You never really move on from the place you were raised."

Levi glanced at me. "You can ignore him. He isn't worth your time."

"Ignore me? I think not. Change is brewing little cousin, and if your mate wants a chance, she should know the truth."

Levi slammed his fist on the table, knocking over several shot glasses. "Shut up."

"What's going to happen when you go down? Hopefully, I'll get to have her first—that is unless something happens to her before then…"

"You son of a bitch." Levi was out of his seat, his eyes solid black as he lunged at Martin. Levi punched him, launching him through the air and into a table. The impact caused the solid wood to split into two. "I told you to shut up."

Levi walked back over to me, grabbing my hand. "Let's go."

"What the hell was that all about?" I stopped short when we reached the sidewalk.

"Nothing."

"I want the truth." I reluctantly let him pull me along, too shaken up to fight.

Levi shifted uncomfortably.

"She deserves it," Owen said from behind us.

Levi let out a deep breath. "Fine, let's go back to our place."

I looked at Hailey and she nodded. I needed answers.

***

Settled on a couch with a cup of coffee, I got ready for what I figured would be some seriously heavy information. Something felt almost humorous about the situation. I was sitting around with a bunch of paranormal creatures drinking coffee. Levi paced around the room. I knew he didn't want to share this stuff with me, but I was done being left in the dark. If he wanted me in his life, he was going to have to start keeping me informed.

"You don't have to worry." Levi stopped pacing long enough to kneel down in front of me. This was going to be bad—really bad.

"Spill it, Levi."

He put his hands on my legs, looking me right in the eye. "You heard what they talked about at the meeting. The Blackwell's are trying to usurp us."

Usurp? I'd never heard Levi speak so formally.

"Aren't they always trying to seize power? This isn't new, is it?" When I'd been kidnapped over the summer, my captors made it seem that way.

"Yes, and no." He looked away for a moment before turning his attention back to me. "They've always wanted power, but they've never actually attempted to take it before. Or at least not in my lifetime."

"We think someone on the inside is leaking information. It seems like the Blackwell's are going to strike soon." Jared took the seat Levi vacated on the couch next to me.

"And you think they're going to come after me, right?" I said the words I knew Levi didn't want to say.

"You're safe, Al. I swear."

"Only if I stay with you." I said it quietly, but knew everyone in the room could hear.

"Yes." His eyes never left my face.

"What does your cousin have to do with this?" No longer wanting my coffee, I set it aside.

"He hates me for being the heir to the throne. He's power hungry."

"Do you think he's working with the Blackwell's then?"

"Maybe. I don't know what he'd have to gain though." Levi still made complete eye contact. I guess he was trying to let me know he was telling me everything.

I reached out and touched his shoulder. He was trying to put me at ease, but at the moment he also needed comforting. He was worried. "Maybe it's not to gain anything, but to hurt you. Jealousy can be a powerful thing."

"Yes, it can."

"I assume by the fact that you're on your knees that you really think someone might come after me again."

"Yes." The one word answers should have annoyed me, but at least he was being honest.

"That's why I have you guys in all of my classes. I'm always being watched, aren't I?"

"Only from a distance. And no one violates your privacy. Hailey lives with you so it isn't necessary."

"But if Hailey wasn't living with me…"

"If you weren't living with Hailey, you'd be living with Levi." Jared always spoke so bluntly.

"What if I don't want to be watched?"

"You have no choice. You're too important." Levi stood up. Jared moved, letting Levi sit back down next to me.

"When can I see my mom? Will it ever be safe, or will I be putting her in danger?" I'd been looking at things in the short term, but I doubted anything would be resolved anytime soon. I wasn't sure how I felt about it. Part of me wanted to go back to New York, but most of me didn't.

"We're going to take care of it. My dad already has some serious leads. It's just a matter of time." Jared's voice sounded a little distant. I knew he wished he were a bigger part of the effort.

"They don't want to kill me though, right? I mean doesn't that defeat the purpose? If they kill me, you can just take another mate."

Levi put a hand under my chin and made me look at him. "You make it sound like a business dealing. Do you realize what losing you would do to me?"

"I'm just saying that they probably want to kidnap me but not kill me." I couldn't believe I was saying it so matter-of-factly, but in some ways it made things easier.

"Don't. Just don't. If anyone took you from me again…I can't even think about it." His voice sounded scratchy.

"Trust me. I'm not letting myself get kidnapped again."

"We're going to keep you safe." Hailey put a hand on my arm. "Remember that."

"Are you going to start telling me stuff? Keeping me in the loop?"

Levi searched my face. "Do you really want me to? Do you really want to know more?"

"Yes," I said confidently. "I need to know."

"Okay, I will."

"You can't be serious." Jared kicked a game controller that was lying on the floor.

"I am. If she wants to know, she deserves to know."

"Good." I leaned my head back. Between meeting Martin, and hearing Levi actually say I was in danger, I didn't think I could take much more. "Does anyone want to take us home?"

"You girls can always stay here…" It sounded like Levi was just going through the motions. He didn't actually expect us to stay.

"I think you know the answer."

"Fine, I'll take you guys back."

Twenty minutes later, I was slipping between the soft sheets of my bed. I couldn't help but look out the window before I lay down. I wondered who was out there watching me, and if it was only Levi's people. For all I knew, there was a Blackwell sitting out there in the dark too. I pulled my blankets tightly around me. I'd spent so much time focused on whether I wanted to get back together with

Levi, that I hadn't been seriously thinking about the danger I was in.

"Are you okay?" Hailey paused with her hand on the light switch.

"I'm fine." I wasn't sure who I was lying to more, Hailey or myself.

CHAPTER NINE

Knowing exactly how much danger I was in didn't change the fact that I still had to go to class. My second week of college wasn't that different from the first. The only real change was that I started my organic chemistry lab.

Jared waited for me outside of my dorm. He smiled when he saw me.

"I'm guessing you have lab too?" I started walking, knowing he'd follow.

"Nope. I couldn't get into it. I'm just keeping you company on the way over."

A few days earlier, I would have told him to get lost, but now I found his presence comforting.

"Are you saying that you guys couldn't override a schedule? You're losing your touch."

"Well, we figured it wasn't that big of a deal. How much trouble can you get into for a few hours of lab, right?"

"Don't remind me. I can't believe lab's starting already."

"I thought you liked this stuff."

"I do. I mean I like learning about it, but that doesn't mean I want to spend three hours in a lab."

Jared laughed. "Good luck with it. I have mine tomorrow." I couldn't imagine Jared in a lab.

We reached the modern glass building that housed the Organic Chemistry lab. It looked out of place amongst the mostly stone buildings of the quad. "Thanks. See ya."

I walked into lab, which was really a series of rooms. I took a lab manual from the pile and found an empty stool. Of all of my classes, this lab made me the most nervous. I was good at listening to lectures and spitting it all back out on exams and in papers. It was something different to actually have to perform experiments. Results never seemed to turn out like they were supposed to. I was sure this would be a lot harder than my science labs in high school.

"Allie, hey."

I glanced up from flipping through the manual. Nick, the guy from the house party, took the stool next to me. "Hi, Nick."

"I didn't know you were in Orgo."

"Yeah, I guess I can say the same thing to you."

"I'm glad you're here. I hate having to find lab partners."

I guess that meant we were working together. I didn't mind, though. Searching for a partner wasn't high on my to-do list. "Me too."

Our TA came in and introduced himself. I expected he wouldn't be like a regular professor, but I was surprised to see he was wearing jeans and a t-shirt.

"Hi guys. Welcome to Organic Chemistry Lab. I'd tell you this was going to be fun, but then I'd be lying." He paused, probably hoping for laughs. He didn't get any.

"Basically, we'll be doing an experiment each week. Just follow your lab manual, and if you have any questions or problems, let me know. Oh, and don't forget to turn in your prelab questions at the start of each class. If there aren't any questions, you can go ahead and check out your first experiment."

I tried not to let the lab intimidate me. It's not like I'd never seen the equipment before, but I'd heard so many horror stories about organic chem.

"Are you premed?" Nick sorted through the equipment on the table.

"Definitely not."

He put down the beaker he was holding. "Really? You're taking this because you want to?"

I laughed. "I guess that makes me a nerd?"

"You couldn't be a nerd if you tried." His eyes raked over me in a way that made me a little bit uncomfortable.

"Nerds have to look a certain way?" I picked up my manual, trying to read over the instructions.

"Yes. I mean anyone can be nerdy, but it takes a lot to be a nerd."

I laughed again. "If you say so."

I tried to focus on the experiment. After measuring several compounds and heating the chemicals in the sand bath, I hoped to have the desired result.

Three grueling hours later, we were done.

"That wasn't so bad." Nick started to clean up.

"I think these things usually start out easy and then get harder." I walked up the front to check out with the T.A.

Nick followed, and we headed outside. Jared was waiting for me by the entry. He glared at Nick. "Hey, Allie, you ready?"

"Sure, see you next week." I waved to Nick.

"See you around." Nick was definitely disappointed as we walked away.

"Who's the kid?" Jared pulled the straps of his backpack away from him.

"My lab partner."

"I'm glad Levi didn't pick you up."

"Pick me up? Do you really have to call it that?"

"What would you prefer?"

"Meet me."

"Okay, I'm glad Levi didn't meet you."

"You always make Levi sound like this crazy, jealous person, but he's never acted that way."

"It's been a new experience for him. He's never had a reason to be jealous before. He was going to have Natalie fire Alex because he didn't like the way he looked at you." Without saying anything, Jared stopped and held open the door to a coffee shop.

"How'd you know I wanted something?"

"I didn't. Levi suggested it. He said you'd probably want a caffeine fix."

"Sometimes he can even pass as charming." I got in line.

Jared smiled. "So what's going on with you guys?"

"Like you don't know." I turned to look at him. "You want anything?"

"I'll take a coffee."

I ordered Jared his coffee, and I got an iced mocha.

We were back outside before Jared answered me. "Levi seems to think you're back together, but for some reason you're holding sex over him."

I pushed his arm. "For some reason? The last time I slept with him I got quite a surprise." I couldn't believe I was talking sex with Jared.

"What's done is done. I assure you, more sex won't change things—other than Levi's sanity that is."

"His sanity? Because lack of sex has been known to cause insanity?"

"I live with the guy. Trust me, it's causing it. You can't give a guy the night of his life and then take it away from him. It screws with you."

I raised an eyebrow. "Like you know anything about that? Have you ever been with the same girl more than once?"

"Yes."

"I'm not talking about multiple times in a night, or a

weekend."

"Okay, you weren't specific. No."

"You're so disgusting."

"What?" He smirked.

"Forget it."

"You're the one who asked."

"All right, let's change the topic. I was meaning to ask you something." I stopped at a bench. We were getting close to the dorms and this talk could take a while.

Jared sat down next to me, tossing his backpack onto the bench next to him. "We're sitting down for it? This I've got to hear. But if you're trying to come on to me, please don't. You are my best friend's mate."

"Dream on, Jared."

"This isn't fun. I can't even throw it back at you."

I laughed. "I'm not going to come on to you."

"Lay it on me then."

I adjusted my bag in my lap and turned to look at him. "You owe me a favor, and I'm calling it in."

"Okay. What kind of favor?"

"Teach me to fight."

"Teach you to fight? Are you joking?"

"I need to be able to defend myself."

"You can't defend yourself against these enemies."

"I need to be able to try. And if I can't fight off paranormals, I should at least be able to stun them or something."

"Why don't you ask Levi?"

"You know what he'd say. Besides, I want to learn from the best. I heard you were the best."

"Kissing my ass isn't going to help."

"It won't?"

He laughed. "Levi would kill me if he found out."

"I don't care. I need this. Will you help? Somehow I don't think the self-defense classes they offer at the gym are going to cut it."

"Yes and no. I'm willing to help you get in better shape

and teach you some basics, but that's it."

"Better shape? Are you implying I'm not in good shape?" I looked down at my body. No one had ever said anything like that to me before.

He rolled his eyes. "You're hot, Allie. Let's face it, if you weren't with Levi, I'd have had you by now, but that's not what I mean. You do lots of cardio, right?"

"Yes." I ignored his sex comment, figuring that snapping at him wasn't good for my cause. "And I use weights and stuff."

"And stuff? That proves my point. We have to get you in shape."

"Okay. I'm willing to work hard."

"Fine. We'll have to do it when Levi's in class so he won't show up at the gym."

"We're meeting at the gym?"

"In the beginning. When I know you can handle actual training, we'll figure out somewhere else."

"Okay, so when do we start."

"Hmm, tomorrow at two o'clock."

"All right."

"But you better be ready to work hard. I'm not going to baby you."

"I don't want you to. I can handle it." I sat up straighter.

"We'll see. Can we go? As fun as this is, I'd like to get home sometime." Jared stood up, slinging his backpack on in one swift movement.

I rolled my eyes. "It's always a pleasure talking to you."

He grinned. "The feeling's mutual."

***

I could barely eat lunch the next day. Despite all my talk, I was nervous about working out with Jared. I usually could hold my own in sports, but I certainly wasn't a fitness guru.

"Are you ever going to tell me what's up?" Hailey finished the last of her sandwich.

"Only if you promise not to tell Levi."

"Do you really have to say that?"

I took a sip of my water. "I'm meeting Jared at the gym. He's supposed to train me to fight."

"What?" Hailey's eyes nearly bugged out of her head. "Why would you willingly subject yourself to that kind of torture?"

"Because he's the best, besides Levi, and I can't ask Levi."

"I can't argue that Jared's good, but why can't you ask Levi?"

"Don't get me started."

"But I thought things were better with you guys." She picked at the fruit salad on her plate.

"Things are good, but I don't think Levi would approve. He'd just tell me to let him protect me."

"I get it. But if Jared pushes you too far, just let me know. I'll kick his ass for you."

I laughed. "Good to know."

After lunch, I did some studying and then changed for the gym. I opted for a tank with a built in bra and some running shorts. Jared was waiting for me outside the weight room when I got there. He was in shorts and a t-shirt, and I caught more than a few girls checking him out. "It took you long enough."

"Shut up. I'm, what, thirty seconds late?"

"Forty-five."

"Big difference."

"Hey, you're the one who wants my help. The least you can do is be on time."

"Don't forget you're returning a favor."

"Yes, and that my best friend would kill me if he knew I was doing this. I still don't get why you don't ask him—and don't give me those stupid excuses again."

"Fine Jared, I admit it. I just love getting sweaty with

you, and since we can't have sex, this is the best I can get."

He laughed. "All right, let's get sweaty then."

"So where do we start?"

"Right over there." He pointed to an empty bench.

"Aren't we going to use the machines?"

"No. We don't use machines. If you're working with me, it's free weights only."

"Okay then." I walked over to the bench.

He started off with light weights, going over some fairly simple arm exercises. Then he moved on to abs, legs, and he didn't stop.

"Oh my god. Please tell me this is the last one." I tried to sit up, but my abs protested.

Jared leaned over me. "You're the one who wanted this. Remember that, Princess."

I groaned. "Fine. What's next?"

We were back on arms and I thought I was going to drop. When I thought I couldn't take anymore, he said the words that were music to my ears. "All right, I think that's it for today."

"Seriously? How long have we been here anyway?" I hadn't brought a watch.

He grinned. "Two hours."

"Oh my god, no wonder I'm dead."

"Suddenly wishing you asked Levi, huh?"

"I'm just hoping I can walk tomorrow."

He laughed.

I picked up my water bottle from where I left it on the ground. Before I could take a sip, Jared grabbed it and gulped half of it down.

"Gross," I muttered after he tossed it back to me.

"Drink up, Princess. You don't want to get dehydrated."

I was too thirsty to argue. I managed to avoid touching my mouth to the bottle as I drank some.

He sniggered. "What? Afraid you're going to catch something?"

"Yes."

"I'm going to pretend you didn't actually mean that."

"Pretending is always healthy."

I picked up my keys and ID, and we walked back downstairs. As we reached the bottom, I noticed Michelle. My stomach turned. Other than Levi, she was the last person I wanted to see.

"Hey Allie," Michelle said with a forced smile. "And Jared…" Her smile got more real…the wheels in her head were turning. "Did you guys work out together?"

"No, we just ran into each other," I answered quickly.

"Isn't that a coincidence?" She did a leg stretch right there in the lobby.

"Not really. Levi wants her protected at all times, and I make it my business to know where she is. Let's go." As little as I wanted to listen to Jared, I followed him out.

"See you two around," she called.

"Go to hell." Jared flipped her the finger right as she turned around.

"Okay, what's the story there?"

"What story?"

"I'd bet a lot that you two have history." I fixed my ponytail.

"Perceptive."

"So when did you sleep with her?"

"History has to mean I slept with her?"

"It doesn't?"

"Nope. Bryant did though."

"Really?"

"Uh huh. More than a few times. Dad sent him to Europe before things could get too out of hand, but she blamed him for leaving. She thought she could piss him off by sleeping with me, but I wasn't interested."

"Because she was your brother's ex?"

He turned to look at me. "Do you really think I'll just sleep with anyone?"

I thought about it for a second. "Maybe not

anyone…but most."

"I have standards, plus I don't inbreed."

"Inbreed? Do you really see it that way?"

Jared looked over his shoulder, like he was double checking no one was listening. "If Pterons kept shacking up with each other, we'd end up like the wolves." He cringed as he said it.

"They were in love, weren't they?"

He shrugged. "Who knows? Who cares?"

Maybe Michelle wasn't as much of a brat as I thought. Maybe she was just heartbroken.

"Thanks for the workout…I think."

"You think?"

"We'll see if I can still move tomorrow."

"If you can't, then we're making progress. You're in good shape, but if you want me to teach you any real fighting technique, you're going to have to push yourself harder."

"Harder? Okay, I can do that."

"Good." The way he said it let me know he actually respected me, and that was a lot coming from Jared.

"Bye, Jared."

"Catch you later, Ali-gator."

"You did not just say that."

"I think I did."

"Oh my god, you do have a geeky side."

"What can I say? You must be a geek to bring it out of me."

"You know it." I turned and walked back to the dorm.

CHAPTER TEN

Time had never moved as fast as it did that semester. I was so busy trying to get through classes, go out enough to enjoy the experience, and figure out what in the world was going on with my relationship with Levi, that before I knew it, it was October. It didn't really feel like October. Without the turning of the leaves, it didn't quite feel like fall, but I loved the warm weather. There is something awesome about wearing a tank top and shorts a few weeks before Halloween.

Sometimes it was possible to forget just how much of a mess my life was. A full course load can do that to you. I was managing okay, except for French. Who would have thought an intro class could be so hard? Foreign language just wasn't my thing. Hailey had actually helped quite a bit, but when I asked her to help me with my papers, she just did them for me.

"What? You asked for help."

"Can't you explain how you figured out the tense?"

"I've already tried to explain it five times."

"Fine, thanks anyway."

"Just ask Levi." Hailey got up from my desk chair.

"He's never going to let me live it down."

"Come on, it's not that big of a deal. You're just failing intro French."

I glared at her. "I'm not failing."

"Really? Because that's what I thought you said when you asked for my help."

"Okay, okay. I know I can be melodramatic sometimes. I got a C on my last paper, and I can't end up with anything less than a B in this class."

Hailey picked up my phone and tossed it to me. "Call him. You know he's going to help."

"And hold it over my head."

"So? You two are making out, I'm sure you can handle a tutoring session with him."

"Maybe in a public place…"

Hailey laughed. "Are you more afraid of him or you?"

I shrugged. "Both."

"I'm going to go do laundry. When I get back, I expect you'll have called him."

"Fine, but could you do me a favor and wash these jeans for me?" I picked up a pair from my hamper. "I think I'm obsessed with them."

"Not a problem."

I waited until the door clicked closed before making myself pick up my phone from where it lay on my bed. Finally, I leaned back against the pillow and pressed call.

"Hey, love."

"Hey, Levi."

There was a momentary silence when I tried to get up the nerve to ask. I'm not sure why I was so afraid. I just didn't want to deal with him rubbing it in my face.

"As much as I love listening to you breathe, is there a particular reason you called? Or is it just to hear my voice."

"Very funny. There is a reason."

"I'm listening." I heard a door close, and I figured he'd gone into his bedroom.

I took a deep breath and let the words out. "I need

your help."

"My help? This is going to be interesting."

"Forget it."

"No, no. Come on, you know I'd help you with anything."

"It's French. I'm going to destroy my GPA with freaking intro French."

He laughed. "Have you had dinner yet?"

"This is serious, Levi. Will you help me?"

"Of course, but answer my question."

"No. I haven't eaten." I was never in that much of a rush to go to the dining hall.

"I'll pick you up in twenty minutes. Pizza or Chinese?"

"Neither. I need help with French, not food." Although takeout did sound good.

"And I need food to help you so I'll see you outside in twenty minutes."

He hung up before I could respond.

The door opened, and Hailey walked in with her empty pop-up hamper. "So, I have thirty minutes until I need to move my clothes, want to get dinner?"

"If you were only two minutes earlier, I could have saved myself."

"Saved yourself?" Understanding crossed Hailey's face. "Wait, from Levi?"

"Yeah…evidently he needs takeout to help me with my French."

Hailey sat down on her chair. "Want to come with me to Bruff first? I don't know where everyone else is, and I don't want to eat alone." She referred to the campus dining hall.

"You don't want to eat alone? Wow. I'm impressed you even care."

"Are you coming?"

"Yeah, of course." I might have given her a hard time, but I'd have hated to eat alone during dinner. Sometimes the dining hall seemed the most like high school—social pressure and all.

***

I was a few minutes late meeting Levi, but he didn't seem to care. "Hey, you ready?"

"Yeah, I think I have everything." I patted my bag that was filled with my French book and notebook.

He put a hand on my back, leading me to his car. "So what are we working on exactly?"

I was surprised that he was asking before dinner. I noticed the brown bag in the backseat when I got in.

"A composition about my summer vacation."

"Oh, this is going to be so good."

"I just can't figure this stuff out. I thought my last paper was perfect and I got a C!"

Levi turned to me with mock shock. "A C? Alert the authorities."

I crossed my arms. "Yes, because caring about my grades somehow makes me lame."

"That's not what makes you lame."

"That had better be a joke."

"It is. It is." Levi pulled up out front of his place and parked.

He grabbed the bag of food from the back, and we went inside. I hadn't been over since the night we went to the paranormal bar.

"Is that enough food?" I watched as Levi took out a few containers and placed them on the kitchen table.

"How much were you planning to eat, hon?"

"You know what I mean. There are four of us."

"No, just two."

"Wait, Jared and Owen aren't here?"

Levi smiled. "No, it turns out they both had plans tonight."

I threw my bag down on an empty chair. "Convenient. Very convenient."

"It is, isn't it?" He took two plates down from a cabinet, and pulled out two sets of disposable chopsticks from the paper bag.

"Whatever. Let's eat." I sat down and opened the containers. "Chicken and Broccoli? Veggie Lo Mein?"

"Is there a problem?" He leaned back against the counter.

"How did you know what I like?"

"Wait, you like these?"

"Yes, they're my favorites."

"It looks like we just like the same things."

"Vegetable Lo Mein? You expect me to believe that?"

"Your roommate may or may not have helped out." He took a seat.

"Hailey? Hailey told you?"

"I didn't realize you guys were doing a weekly takeout and movie night without me."

"Yes you did. You definitely did." Levi had asked to join us on more than one occasion.

He shrugged. "I don't remember getting the invitation."

"Because you're not invited. It's girls only."

"I'm not complaining. I wish all of your girls' nights involved you at home with your friends in pajamas." He scooped some food on his plate. "On the other hand, I'd rather you didn't insist on going out to bars without me."

"Do you realize how insane you are?"

"Why? Because I'd rather you not be out in a short skirt with guys throwing themselves at you?" He casually grabbed an egg roll like we were talking about nothing of consequence.

"You can't tell me what to do."

"Did I try to? I only told you my preference."

"All right, let's eat."

"I already am." He bit into the egg roll.

I made myself a plate. "When did you ask Hailey?"

"About your favorite dishes?"

"Yes."

"This morning."

"How'd you know it would come up?" I opened the paper packaging on my chopsticks.

"I didn't think it would be tonight, but I knew you'd come asking for help eventually with a paper due so soon."

"Owen."

"Yes. Can we stop worrying about how I know, and enjoy our dinner?"

"Sure."

"Good. I'd suggest we find a movie, but that's not why you're here."

"Don't remind me." I took a bite.

After finishing our meal and cleaning up, Levi sat down with me at the table. "Let me see what you have so far."

I pushed my notebook over to him. "Is there any reason why you handwrite your papers?"

"Just the first draft, and just French. I type the rest."

"Where's your laptop?"

"In my room. It's too clunky to carry around."

He leaned on his elbow. "You need a light weight one."

"No, I don't. I just need help."

"Fine, let's see if I can read this chicken scratch."

I was about to defend my perfectly neat handwriting when I noticed the playful expression on his face. He was trying to be funny.

"One of these days I'm going to figure out when you're joking."

"Maybe in the next ten years."

He looked down at my paper, and I felt uncomfortable watching him read it. I knew there were tons of mistakes.

I tapped my foot nervously, hoping he wouldn't give me too hard of a time.

He laughed. "You met a boy and ate him?"

"I did not write that!"

"Yes, actually you did. I'm guessing you meant to say you met and went out to eat."

"Of course. Arrh." I put my head in my hands. "Why is it that I can handle every subject but foreign languages? It's like I'm cursed."

"Come on, it's really not that bad. The rest of it looks pretty good. You just need to be careful with your verbs."

"You make that sound easy."

"Okay, why don't we finish up this paper, and then just do some verb exercises."

"Verb exercises? Have you tutored in French before?"

He nodded. "I helped out a little in high school. It was the only way I was allowed to take French."

"You were fluent before high school?"

"Yeah. My dad insisted on it. It's just a family thing. Our kids will have to learn it too."

I'd never heard Levi talk about us having kids. Obviously I knew he had to think about it, because unless he had an heir his line died, but it sounded so strange hearing it from him.

"Okay, let's get this over with." I pulled up my legs and sat with them crossed on the chair.

Levi leaned over me, pointing out all of my mistakes, and showing me how to fix them. "When's this due, anyway?"

"Monday."

"Okay, so you can just type it up later."

"Thanks for the help. I really appreciate it."

"You know I don't mind." Once again, Levi sounded serious. As much as I wanted him to stop messing around sometimes, it was harder to push reality aside when he was this way.

Levi was making me go through the various verb forms of "to be" when my phone rang. "Mind if we take a break? It's Anne."

"Go ahead."

I picked up. "Hey, Anne."

"Hey. You're still at Levi's right?"

"I'm guessing Hailey told you?"

"Yeah, I'm not interrupting anything am I?" she said suggestively.

"Yeah, you're interrupting some hot French studying."

"Hey, you know Levi would be happy to tutor you in other things."

"Don't start."

The look Levi gave me made me think he might have heard her. I hoped not. Either way, he got up and refilled his glass with water.

"Okay, okay. I'm calling because a bunch of us are going to Rock 'n' Bowl."

"Rock 'n' Bowl?"

"Yeah, there's a Cajun band playing that Brandon was raving about the other day."

"Brandon? You've been talking to him more?"

"Yeah, he's in my psych class, remember?"

"Oh yeah."

"Are you in?"

"I don't know. I have an econ test in the morning."

"Don't you know that stuff ridiculously well? And if you don't, why are studying French?"

"I do know it. I just don't want to stay out too late." My responsible side kicked in.

"Then come for an hour or so. We can leave early."

I considered it. Music and bowling sounded a lot better than studying. "Maybe. I'll let you know."

"Okay, bye."

Levi was back in his seat when I hung up. "Rock 'n' Bowl, huh?"

"Have you been there? Is it cool?"

"Yes, I've been there. And it's definitely an experience."

"An experience?"

"Yeah, want to go and find out?" He flipped my pen around in his hand.

"Sure, for a little bit. Could you drive me home kind of early though?" If Levi was going, it would make things easier. We'd gone out as a group a lot, but this was actually the first time since the summer that we'd be arriving somewhere just the two of us.

"Of course. I wouldn't want you too tired for your econ test." He smiled. I knew he was making fun of me, but I refused to let him get a rise out of me.

"Thanks, I appreciate it."

"And, as always, the offer to come back here is on the table."

I shook my head. "You just had to add that in, huh?"

"Come on, you can't blame me."

"All right, I'll let Anne know."

***

Rock 'n' Bowl wasn't at all what I expected. Surprisingly, I didn't mind how closely Levi stuck to my side as we walked inside. He easily moved us through the crowds of people who were drinking beer while listening to the loud music. We found my friends on a lane.

"Here you go." Hailey tossed me a pair of socks.

"Thanks." I caught the rolled up socks. "Wait, you really think I'm going to put on bowling shoes?"

"Of course. I've got your size eight and a half's right here." She gestured to a pair of red and blue bowling shoes.

"Did you get mine too?" Levi held out his hand.

"No. Get your own."

"Fine. I'll be back in a second." He walked off, and I expected it to take a while considering how crowded it was.

"How was your French tutoring?" Anne grinned.

"Thrilling."

She laughed. "Well, he's a lot hotter than any tutor I've ever seen."

"Thanks, Anne. I appreciate that." Of course, he chose that moment to return. Evidently, his charm worked at bowling alleys too. I doubted Levi actually knew what it was like to wait in line.

"Is Jared meeting you here?" Tiffany asked Levi.

"Why? You want to see him?"

I pushed Levi.

"What? I'm sure Jared would love to hear that."

Tiffany blushed. "No. I just wondered since Jared and Owen are usually with you."

"But you didn't ask about Owen."

"Shut up, Levi."

"What?"

I glared at him.

"Fine. Sorry Tiffany."

She looked away. "I was just surprised, that's all."

"We know. Levi's just being his usual self." Hailey's expression mirrored my own.

"Hey, sorry we're late." Nick shot me a smile as he walked over with Brandon.

"It's fine. Allie and Levi just got here." Anne smiled at both of them, but it was obvious she was really paying attention to Brandon. I hadn't realized Nick was coming. This could get awkward.

"Oh, you guys came together?" Nick asked. I didn't know why he was playing dumb. He was well aware that Levi and I were dating.

"Of course we did." Levi pulled me tighter against his side.

"Allie doesn't have to go everywhere with you. You don't own her," he mumbled.

What the hell was Nick doing? Levi took a step towards Nick, pushing me slightly behind him. "No, I don't own her, but I am going to marry her."

"Are you guys done with your pissing contest?" Anne broke the tension. "We came here to bowl."

I shrugged off Levi's arm long enough to change shoes. "All right, let's do this."

Tiffany started us off, then took a seat next to me. "All

right, that wasn't too embarrassing."

I retied the shoelace that had already come undone. "You hit seven pins. I've never hit seven pins."

"Seriously?"

"Okay, I have. With bumpers."

Tiffany laughed.

I suddenly noticed something. "This might be a dumb question, but where's the computer? How do we record our scores?"

Levi bowled a strike and came to sit down next to me. "It's called a pencil and paper, Al. Aren't you the one who likes it old school?"

"You really record it like that?"

"Yes." He smiled. "I told you this would be an experience."

I was definitely the worst bowler there. Anne was incredible. No wonder she wanted to come. She even came close to holding her own against Levi and Hailey—almost. I'm pretty sure Pteron's are good at everything. Neither of them even looked down the lane when they threw their balls. Even Nick, Tiffany, and Brandon left me in the dust. I drowned my humiliation in a couple of beers, and eventually was able to laugh at myself.

We were having so much fun that I didn't realize how late it was getting until Levi put an arm around me. "Hey, Cinderella, if we don't leave soon, you're going to turn into a pumpkin."

I laughed. "It's the coach that turns into the pumpkin, not Cinderella."

"Same difference."

"Is it really that late?" I pulled out my phone and looked at the time. "One? It's one a.m?"

Levi nodded.

"Why didn't you tell me? I have a test at nine!"

"You were having fun. Are you ready to go then?"

"Yes!" I knew it wasn't Levi's fault, but I really needed to get some sleep.

We said goodnight to everyone and Levi walked me out to his car. "On the positive side, you're not drunk. At least you won't be hung over tomorrow."

"No, not hung over. Just falling asleep."

"Just get through the test and take a nap."

"I will after French."

He laughed. "You're such a goody two shoes."

"Not exactly. I just like passing my classes."

"Never change, Al. Please, never change."

I laughed. "I don't plan on it."

***

By the time I finished my economics exam, I could barely keep my eyes open.

"Oh my god." I gathered my stuff and walked out of the classroom.

"What's up, Princess? Think you failed or something?" Jared caught up with me before I reached the hallway.

"Actually no. I think I did all right, but I swear I'm never taking another test after going out again." I pushed open the door.

Jared glared at a guy who bumped into him. "Don't swear about promises you can't keep."

"Oh, I'm going to keep it."

"You've got four years of college ahead of you. It's going to happen again."

I rolled my eyes. "Well, all I want to do right now is go home and go back to sleep. Damn French."

"You could always skip."

"I'm lucky I'm passing."

"That's where Levi comes in, right?"

"Yeah, yeah." I looked away. I didn't want to see the smirk I knew would be on Jared's face.

I turned back and he didn't disappoint. "Did his French expertise win you over?"

"Not quite, but he did help."

"What's holding you back? I thought you were over everything."

"I still don't know if I can trust him."

Jared looked me straight in the eye. "You can."

"Thanks for your unbiased opinion."

"Always at your service."

"You know, you're not as bad as I thought you were." I tried to bite back a smile, but it came out anyway.

"Wait, are you trying to give me a backhanded compliment?"

"Just accept it before I take it back."

He pulled up his sunglasses so I could see his eyes. "You're not as bad as I thought either."

"Good."

"So, I'll see you for training tomorrow?"

"Yes, boss."

"Hey, you're the one who wants the help."

I smiled. "Admit it. You like it."

"I like that you're not nearly as weak and pathetic as I thought."

"Let's stop while we're ahead here."

He laughed. "Okay, enjoy French and your nap."

"Will do. Tell Levi I said 'hi.'"

Jared stopped and looked at me. "Okay, I will."

I met up with Owen and prepared myself for fifty minutes of French hell.

CHAPTER ELEVEN

Jared picked me up in his black Mustang convertible. "Nice wheels."

"I'm glad you think so." He pulled away from the curb before I'd even buckled my seatbelt.

"Where are we going?" He finally thought I was ready to do some training outside of the gym. I wasn't sure if I was more nervous or excited.

"Just down to the levee. It should be empty at this time of night."

Meeting Jared at the gym was one thing. Sneaking off with him late at night felt different. It's not like Levi had to worry about something happening between us, that would be the last thing that would ever occur, but I knew he wouldn't like the idea of me learning to fight.

Jared parked, and I got out. I was dressed in black yoga pants, and a tank with a sweatshirt over it. Jared was in shorts and a t-shirt. Pterons never seemed to get cold.

"Okay, I'm ready." I braced myself. I figured Jared wouldn't actually hurt me.

He laughed. "You look ready to fight in battle. What do you think we're doing here?"

"You said you'd teach me to fight."

"I said I'd teach you to defend yourself."

"Fine, so where do we start?"

"First, you need to listen, and listen closely."

I put a hand on my hip. I hadn't dragged myself out in the dark to listen.

"You ready?"

"I'm listening."

"You are never going to be able to fight a Pteron or other paranormal head on."

"Come on."

"I'm being serious. You can't. Even the strongest human is too weak. And face it, Princess, you aren't the strongest human." He touched my arm as though that proved something.

"Then what do you suggest?"

"First, remember to use the old tried and true methods."

"Meaning?"

"A good kick to the nuts is going to give you a nice head start."

I glanced at that region of Jared without thinking. "Get serious."

He caught the direction of my gaze "Don't even think of trying it out on me. Anyway, most of us have such good reflexes, that you wouldn't get the chance, but it's worth remembering."

"Okay, so what if that doesn't work or isn't an option?"

"You have to take your opponent by surprise and go after their weaknesses."

"Do Pteron's even have weaknesses?" I certainly didn't know of any.

"We have one."

"What?"

"Listen, this isn't something we ever admit, and I shouldn't even be telling you." He studied his feet. He really didn't want to be having that conversation.

"You have to tell me."

"I will. But only because I want you alive, for Levi's sake."

I glared at him. I was sure he could see it in the dim light. "Nice, very nice."

"Do you want to know or not?"

"I want to know."

"Then play nice." He smirked.

"Please, Jared. Be kind enough to share your wisdom."

He laughed. "All right." He pulled off his t-shirt.

"As much as being in our Pteron form makes us stronger, it also exposes us." He extended his large wings.

I waited. I still had no idea what the weakness could be.

"Come behind me." I listened and moved behind him.

"Put a hand on my back, right where my wings meet."

I hesitated. Touching his wings felt almost intimate, as strange as that sounds.

"Just do it, Allie. We don't have all night."

I reached out a hand and placed it right where he told me to.

"If you pushed your hand up right now, you'd immobilize me."

"Seriously?"

"Yes seriously. And I wouldn't appreciate it if you tried it."

"Just by pushing up?"

"Yes. Of course, Pteron's guard that spot so it's not going to be easy to get to it, but it's probably the only way you'd ever take down a Pteron."

"Did you bring me out here just to show me that?"

He retracted his wings and pulled on his t-shirt. "I appreciate your interest, but you really have to stop coming on to me."

"Shut up. I just thought we'd be doing more."

"I just revealed the biggest Pteron secret, and you want more?"

"Fine. I'm sorry. Thank you. I really do appreciate it."

"Good. Now let's get you back to your dorm."

"All right."

I got back into Jared's car for the short ride back. I stared out the window, enjoying the way the street lights lit up the beautiful homes and live oaks along the way.

Jared parked, got out, and leaned against the door. "Sweet dreams."

"You too."

"Do me a favor?" I figured it was just going to be one of his annoying jokes.

"Sure."

"Tell Tiffany I said 'hi.'"

"Remember the rules."

"The rules don't prevent me from saying hello."

I laughed. "I guess not. Good night."

I went back inside, and hoped I'd never have to use the trick Jared showed me. In the pit of my stomach, I knew I probably would.

***

I'd never been in Owen's truck before, but when he offered to give me a ride down to the hotel, I jumped on it.

"Thanks for the ride." I put on my seat belt and smiled at Owen. It didn't surprise me at all that he drove a Toyota Tacoma. He kind of seemed like a truck guy.

"Not a problem." He turned down the volume on the Linkin Park song currently blaring from the speakers.

It was strange. I'd gotten to know Jared so well over the past months but still felt like Owen was a mystery. I would have expected the opposite.

"Are you excited to see your dad?" He glanced over.

"Yeah, but his call surprised me." I hadn't seen my dad since the whole ring incident. I had no clue what brought him back to town after so much time. My gut told me it wasn't good.

"I bet. You should have seen your face when you listened to the message."

Dad rarely called me, so to get a message from him in the middle of the day had been surprise enough. Discovering he was in town, at the hotel, and wanted to meet up with me bordered on shocking. "Well, at least it will be good to see him." That was true. I missed him. I just hoped he'd be his usual clueless self and wouldn't notice the ruby ring on my left ring finger.

Owen pulled up out front of the hotel. "I'm going to park and hang around for a bit. Give me a call if you want a ride home."

"You make it sound like I could just go home alone."

He shrugged. "Technically, you could."

"But someone would follow me."

"Yeah, but you wouldn't be with them."

"I'll keep that in mind. Thanks for the ride." I walked into the hotel slowly. I couldn't shake the feeling that this wasn't going to be a pleasant father-daughter lunch.

My dad was waiting for me at a table in the dining room. He got up as soon as he saw me. "Hey, sweetie."

"Hey, Dad." I hugged him. I didn't pull away as quickly as I usually would. It felt nice to be hugged by him. I took a step back. "You look great."

"Thanks." He smiled.

"You've lost weight." He had, or maybe he was just trimmer or something. He was never overweight really, but now he looked like he was in good shape.

"You can thank my girlfriend for that. She's been on my back about eating and exercising."

"Girlfriend? Why are you and mom so into dating all of a sudden?"

"Your mother is dating?"

I rolled my eyes. "Yes. I thought we discussed this." In our brief conversations, the topic had still managed to come up.

"That's enough about your mom. How are you?" He

pulled out a chair for me.

"I'm doing all right. College has definitely been an adjustment though."

"I bet. Are classes going well?"

"Mostly. I hate French, but I'm getting through it."

"French? Why didn't you just take Spanish?"

"I wanted to try something different." I unfolded my napkin and put it on my lap.

"You seem to be all about trying new things, nowadays."

"What's that supposed to mean?"

He looked away and took a long drink from his water. "Are you ready to tell me why you decided to change schools? It's because of the boy, isn't it?"

"His name is Levi, and sort of." I'd already decided that was the easiest answer, especially now that we were somewhat dating again.

"What does 'sort of' mean? Either it was because of him or it wasn't." Dad finished off his water before signaling the waiter for a refill.

"It means I wanted to see where things went."

"And where did they go?"

"What's going on, Dad? What's with the interrogation?"

"Interrogation? You're the one who decided to throw away my deposit at Princeton to transfer schools for a boy you'd just met."

"Deposit? It's the money you care about?"

"Money doesn't grow on trees."

"Where's all this coming from?"

Dad ran a hand through his hair. He was nervous. "Are you sure you don't want to get back with Toby?"

I took a sip of my water. I needed to calm down before I answered. "Toby? We've been over for months. What does Toby have to do with anything?"

"We're going under."

"What's going under?"

"The company, Allie."

I gripped the table for support. "How?"

"We had two bad quarters, and we lost several investors. I thought I had Tyler Henderson on board, but he made it clear he was only interested in helping someone who had the same interests."

"Are you saying he won't invest because I dumped Toby?"

"I'm saying he won't invest unless you two work it out."

"Well, we're not going to."

"Tulane's not cheap."

"Don't pin this on me. Princeton would have been just as expensive."

"You would be back with Toby."

"No, I wouldn't. And don't worry about tuition. I'll figure out loans or something."

"Even if you did, that doesn't help the bigger picture. This is about a lot more than tuition, it's the whole business. I'm not asking you to marry him. Just spend some time with Toby and see if you can't work something out."

I'd had enough. First, all the crap with Levi, and now my dad? No one was cornering me again. "I've lost my appetite." I stood up to leave.

"Allie, wait."

I ignored him and walked out of the restaurant. I picked up my phone and called Owen. "Can you take me home?"

"Levi's going to give you a ride."

"Perfect. I'll meet him outside."

"No, I'm here." Levi materialized out of nowhere. He'd probably been hanging out at the bar.

Just then, Dad walked out of the restaurant. He'd probably realized I wasn't coming back. "Allie, we're not done."

"Yes, we are." I turned to Levi. "Please get me out of

here."

Dad pleaded. "Allie, we need to talk. You've got the wrong idea."

"The wrong idea? You pretty much just told me to whore myself out to save your company, or am I wrong?"

"Lower your voice. I didn't say anything of the sort. I was just giving you information."

Levi wrapped an arm around my waist, and I was glad for it. I needed any support I could get. "You know I love you, and I care about your company, but you just crossed a line you shouldn't have. I don't want to say anything I'm going to regret, so I'm leaving."

"Allie."

"No."

Dad looked at Levi. "Can you please give us a moment?"

"Sorry, I think I better get her home." Wow, he'd seriously just stood up to my dad. I let Levi lead me out to his car.

"You want to tell me what that was all about?" Levi asked when we were about halfway uptown.

"You didn't get it from the part you heard?"

"I'm guessing he didn't actually want to use you as a prostitute."

"He wanted me to get back with Toby to help his business."

"What?" Levi's hands tightened on the wheel.

"I know my dad didn't really mean it. He's just desperate. He got the company from his dad—who always called him a failure. He's just trying to save it."

"Are you okay?"

"Yeah, just mad."

"I'm guessing you don't want to talk about it?" He put a hand on my arm.

"Good guess."

"Want to grab some lunch?"

"I'd love some."

"All right, I know just the place."

"Where?"

"Semolina's. It's good Italian."

"Sounds perfect."

I couldn't believe that I'd just run away from my dad and to Levi. Sometimes life just seemed so complicated.

***

"Come on guys, this is serious." Anne crossed her arms, glaring at us from across the table.

"How can Halloween costumes be serious?" I tried to pay attention to the economics notes in front of me, but my mind was still on my conversation with Dad.

"We need to come up with the ultimate costumes. I don't want anything lame."

"Then come up with one. Why do we all have to have matching costumes?" Hailey used a clip to pull back her hair.

"Because then everyone knows we're together. It's more fun."

"All right, what ideas do you have?" Tiffany set aside her laptop. We'd fallen into a routine of all studying together at the same table at one of the campus coffee shops.

"I was thinking Disney Princesses. We can make them all cute and slutty. Obviously, Hailey could be Ariel, I'd be Jasmine, Allie could be Belle, and Tiffany can have her pick of the blondes."

I laughed. "Oh, how can Tiffany choose between Cinderella and Sleeping Beauty?"

Hailey shook her head. "No way. You couldn't pay me to dress up as a love sick mermaid. Next."

"Fine, what do you guys want to be?"

"Flappers?" I suggested. "I dressed up as one sophomore year, and it was fun."

"We need to save those for the Prohibition party. I

heard it's epic." Anne played with the straw in her iced coffee.

"What party isn't epic?" I asked, biting back a smile. "But, hey, I tried."

Anne ate a tiny bite of her blueberry muffin. "And it was a great suggestion."

"Pirates. Why don't we go as pirates?" Tiffany took a sip of her coffee.

"I like that." Hailey smiled.

"Same here. It's classic," I agreed.

"Pirates…we can work with that. Let's go as sexy pirates." Anne was probably already designing our costumes in her head.

"I never said sexy…" Tiffany got a panicked expression on her face.

"It went without saying."

I leaned over to whisper to Tiffany. "Don't worry. I'm not wearing anything too slutty either."

"But remember…Allie's definition of slutty probably differs from yours," Hailey ribbed.

Before I could throw a sarcastic comment back to Hailey, Brandon pulled over a chair, throwing an arm over Anne's shoulder. She stiffened. I wondered what had gone down between them. "Hey guys."

"Hey." I gave him a wave.

"What are you all up to?"

"What does it look like?" Hailey played with my little highlighter tabs. I resisted the urge to grab the pink ones from her. I really loved those things.

"You weren't studying."

"We're planning our Halloween costumes, if you must know." Anne crossed her arms again.

"What are you going as?"

"It's a surprise."

"Okay when did you two sleep together?" Hailey said the words on my mind—only I never would have said them out loud.

Tiffany spit out her coffee, and Anne turned beet red.

"I'm going to go…" Brandon excused himself quickly.

"Was that necessary?" I asked.

Hailey shrugged. "Sorry, it just came out."

Anne sighed. "We haven't had sex, but we got close last weekend."

"When?"

She looked down at the table. "We met up at the Boot…don't ask."

"Okay…" Hailey, Tiffany, and I looked at each other.

Anne quickly brought the conversation back to costumes. "So, who wants to go shopping for supplies tomorrow?"

"Supplies?" I closed my econ book, realizing there was no way I was getting back to it.

Anne pushed away the rest of her muffin, letting us know it was up for grabs. "For our costumes. I heard there's an awesome costume shop on Magazine Street."

"I'll go." Hailey seemed strangely excited.

"Okay cool. You get out at two tomorrow, right?" It was a testament to how much the four of us hung out that we knew each other's schedules.

"Yup, we can take the streetcar to my parents' house and get my car." Hailey finally released my tabs.

"Okay, great." Anne was immediately back to herself again. Considering how messed up things were with Levi, I couldn't judge anyone else for their relationships.

CHAPTER TWELVE

"I can't believe I'm actually going out in this." I checked my reflection one last time in the mirror. The pirate costumes Anne designed were actually cute—but also very revealing. A short mini dress was the base of the costume, and with my long legs it looked even shorter. Add in black boots and a low-cut top with laces, and it screamed sex.

"You and me both." Tiffany finished putting on eyeliner. "No one from home would believe I'd ever dress this way."

"You'll have to post a picture tonight." Hailey laughed. "If it makes you feel better, if we run into my brother, he'll make fun of me for the rest of my life."

"Would Owen really care?" Anne asked. She was already waiting impatiently at the door.

"Yes. He still thinks I'm a little kid. Levi and Jared do too."

"An older brother is better than a younger one. Mine is the most annoying kid alive." Tiffany replaced the eyeliner in her makeup bag.

I slipped in gold hoop earrings. "At least you guys have

siblings. I'm an only child."

"You didn't like it?" Anne asked. She had two younger sisters.

"It gets lonely."

"Levi's an only child too, right? I guess you guys have each other now."

I forced a laugh. "Speaking of Levi, I need you guys to swear you won't let me go home with him if I get drunk."

"What? You think you've lost your willpower?" Hailey adjusted her top one last time.

"I plan on drinking. Hopefully, we won't run into them and it won't be a problem."

Anne nodded solemnly. "I won't let you."

"Thanks." We all grabbed our purses and headed out.

We waited on the grassy median for the streetcar. Based on the crowd around us, Bourbon Street was going to be hopping. When the streetcar stopped, I had my money ready. I inserted the exact change into the machine, smiling to myself when I remembered my first time on a streetcar. It was the night of my first kiss with Levi.

The streetcar was packed to capacity, so we all found straps to hold onto. If the car was that crowded uptown, it was only going to get worse. Way before Canal Street, the car ignored the other stops because there was absolutely no room.

"This is crazy," Anne said as we pushed through the crowds.

"You think so?" Hailey smiled. "Wait until Mardi Gras."

"I can't imagine." I looked down at my outfit self-consciously when I caught a group of guys staring at us.

"Where should we go first?" Hailey asked once we reached Bourbon.

"Let's do Tropical Isle. I want a Hand Grenade." Tiffany uncharacteristically made the first suggestion.

"Sounds awesome." I was just glad we had a destination.

We didn't make it that far. "Hey, guys!" A group of girls from our floor called to us. Sometimes New Orleans felt more like a small town than a city. It was impossible to go anywhere without running into someone you knew. I didn't think it was a bad thing.

"Hey! Up here!" A group of guys on a balcony yelled down at us. "Show us some titties if you want some beads."

Hailey rolled her eyes. "Do they really think we're that desperate for cheap plastic beads?"

Anne gave them the finger.

"Over here." I covered my face with my hands as one of my floor mates, Amy, lifted her shirt.

Anne laughed, so I looked up. Amy had a tank top underneath.

"Get a life!" Amy yelled.

"Nice one," a few of us said at once.

"Did you really think I was going to flash them?" Amy was definitely insulted.

I shrugged. "I don't know. I hoped not."

"For future knowledge, I'm not a skank."

"All right, duly noted."

"We're going to head over to Oz, you guys want to come?" Amy asked.

"No thanks," Tiffany answered quickly.

I laughed. "We're good."

"You weren't interested in hitting up a gay bar on Halloween?" Hailey teased Tiffany.

Tiffany laughed. "That place is crazy even on a normal night. Plus, the last time we were there a guy from my American lit class was dancing. That was a sight I don't need to see again."

We all laughed and decided to check out some more bars. We continued down Bourbon Street.

"Those are incredible vampire costumes!" Anne pointed to two guys with long fangs and black capes.

I tried to get a closer look at their eyes as we passed

them, and they definitely had the rings Levi had told me about. I was sure the fangs were real. I shivered. Halloween was a lot scarier when you knew monsters actually existed.

***

"Why, hello Matey." Levi's voice came as a whisper right behind me.

I spun around. "Hi." The word stuck in my throat as I took him in. Dressed in a black tank and jeans, his clothing didn't hint at a costume, but his wings did. I looked past him and noticed Jared and Owen dressed identically.

"We're fallen angels."

"Ah, those are really realistic wings." I reached out to touch one but held back.

"You can touch me, Al. You always can."

I shivered knowing he meant more than his wings.

"Wow, awesome costumes!" Anne walked around the boys, taking them in.

"Hailey has one of these costumes too, but I guess she thought being a slutty pirate was cooler," Owen taunted.

Hailey glared. "We're sexy pirates, not slutty."

"I don't care what you are. You can make me walk your plank anytime." Jared said it to all of us, but his eyes were fixed entirely on Tiffany. She blushed. I resisted the urge to reprimand Jared. It might make Tiffany feel weirder.

"Just be glad he's not asking you to walk *his* plank." Hailey grinned.

"Ugh, okay, no need to give me that image." I rolled my eyes.

"Want something to drink?" Levi was right next to me, his lips inches from mine. I leaned into him, already a little tipsy. Looking at the "Real Levi" was making it hard for me to resist him.

"Get me my usual." Levi still hadn't told me what was in my drink, but it was sweet, strong, and so good.

"Someone's getting some tonight," Jared mumbled, following Levi away. Levi heard and turned back to grin at me.

"No, he's not." Anne crossed her arms. The effect had her cleavage spilling out ever so slightly from her top. Owen's eyes widened. If she noticed, she didn't show it. "Allie made us promise not to let her go home with him if she was drunk, and she's drunk."

"I'm going to help them with the drinks." Owen stumbled away.

I put down my empty glass on a nearby table. "I'm not drunk."

"You're getting there."

"It doesn't matter. I don't want to go home with him."

"Sure…" Hailey rolled her eyes.

The guys returned and Levi took his spot next to me again.

"You make a good looking pirate." He handed me my drink. "I'd go hunting for buried treasure with you anytime."

I looked down at my tight, black top with the white ruffles and red ties, but knew it was the length of the black skirt that probably had his attention. "You'd like it better if it were all red, wouldn't you?"

"I like you in more than red." He paused, playing with the laces on the top. "And in less."

His eyes devoured me, and I sipped my drink.

"I didn't expect to see you guys here." We were on Bourbon Street, and I'd heard most of the upperclassman hung out on Frenchman Street on Halloween.

"I knew you'd be around here somewhere."

"So you came looking for me?" I took another few sips of my drink. It was easy to drink fast.

"Yes. You wouldn't tell me what your costume was, but I knew it would be something I'd have to see."

"In other words, you didn't want me dressed this way without you?"

"Can you blame me?" He moved closer.

"I can say the same about you."

He cracked a smile. "You don't like me out with my wings showing?"

"Not without me." I bit my lip.

"Wow, I had no idea they had that effect on you. So nice to know."

"I'm not going to even try to deny it." I finished my drink.

"Want another?"

"Yes." I didn't hesitate with my answer. I followed him over to the bar, hoping to hear what he ordered. Unfortunately, he just asked the bartender for the same thing. With a crowd that big, I'd have expected the girl to have forgotten—but I don't think it's easy to forget anything about Levi.

He handed me the drink, and we walked back to where our friends had migrated to. Levi sat down on a bar stool pushed against the wall.

"You look so good with your wings." I reached out and touched one, but he shifted, moving it from my reach.

"If you want to touch them, you have to come closer."

"I am close. If I get any closer, I'll be on your lap."

"You say it like it's a bad thing."

"It's a very bad thing." I gave up trying to reach his wing and put my hand on his leg instead.

"I disagree. It's good." His heated look nearly undid me.

Distracted, I felt the tickle of a wing brushing against me as he pulled me up on his lap to straddle him. "Have you ever…"

"Have I ever what?" He gave me an amused smile.

"I'm the only girl you've been with who knows what you really are, right?" I touched his wings.

"Uh huh."

"So you've never done it with your wings out, right?"

He laughed. "No, I haven't." His hand settled on my

very exposed leg.

"Could we?"

"Come home with me, Al, and we can do anything you want."

"Does it have to be at your place? The hotel is closer."

"It is, isn't it?" he whispered next to my ear. "Ready to go?"

"Maybe."

"Whoa. Slow down there." Anne helped me down off his lap.

Levi reluctantly let go but he spun on Anne. "Is there a reason you're interrupting us?"

"Yes. Allie's not going anywhere with you." She put a hand on her hip and scowled.

"It's okay—"

She cut me off. "No. You told me not to let you go home with him, and I'm keeping my word."

I smiled. Anne definitely was tough and a good friend. With some distance between us, I was starting to realize just how big of a mistake I was about to make.

"If she wants to come home with me, she will." Levi was on his feet.

"I think it's time to go." Hailey grabbed my arm and Anne's. Tiffany nodded.

I glanced behind me. Levi's eyes were starting to turn black. Jared and Owen were at his side, trying to calm him down.

"Wow, if looks could kill, I'd be dead." Anne shivered. She didn't know the half of it.

"I'm sorry I brought you into that."

"No, it's totally fine…but I have a feeling you're the reason for the anger problem. A guy can only take so much." She gave me a knowing look. Was she really blaming his anger on sexual frustration?

"Yeah, I don't know." My stomach rumbled.

"Is anyone else hungry?" I asked.

"Yes," everyone said at once.

"How about beignets?" Tiffany adjusted her top, probably trying to get more coverage than it actually provided.

"Café Du Monde?" I asked, even though I didn't have to.

Hailey glanced at her watch. "What better way to end a night?"

"Exactly."

I was already dreaming about the hot, sweet beignets before we got there.

***

"I don't think there's a better drunk food." I took another bite of my beignet.

"I agree. It just works. Add in the coffee and it's perfect." Tiffany took a sip of her chicory coffee.

"So, what did you guys think of your first Halloween in New Orleans?" Hailey asked.

"It was definitely my best yet." Anne polished off her beignet.

"I know I already said it, but I'm sorry about Levi." I hoped Anne wasn't mad at me.

"Don't worry about it. I really didn't mind."

"You know Jared really well, right?" Tiffany looked at Hailey.

"Yeah. I've known him my whole life." Hailey glanced at me. We were both wondering where this conversation was going.

Tiffany concentrated on her mug. "Is he really like that, or is it an act?"

"Do you mean is he really a perverted jerk?" Hailey could be so blunt.

"I was thinking more whether he always so forward?"

I decided to take over. "Yes. That's just him. He's not a bad guy, just a player."

"Oh." Tiffany looked pensive.

"Why are you asking, Tiff? Are you interested in him?" Anne asked the question we were all thinking.

"No! Of course not. I was just trying to figure him out."

"He likes you." I figured I'd be honest.

Tiffany blushed. "He does not."

"He told me to tell you 'hi' the other night."

"The other night? When were you with Jared at night?" Anne leaned forward.

I tried to think fast, but Tiffany spared me. "Did he really say that?"

I smiled. "Yeah. He's a player, and you should keep your distance, but he definitely has a crush."

"A crush? Can you imagine what Jared would say if he heard you say that?" Hailey laughed.

"It's the truth."

"It's flattering. I mean, I know nothing's ever going to happen, but you have to admit, he's really hot."

"No question. He's hot." Anne sipped her coffee.

"But you aren't actually interested, right?" Hailey asked.

"No. Definitely not. He's not my type."

"Okay, good."

I hoped she was being honest. I didn't want to watch him hurt another one of my friends.

CHAPTER THIRTEEN

Time didn't slow down after Halloween. I was having fun, but sometimes the stress was hard to take. It only got worse in November knowing finals were getting closer. I never imagined it would be so hard to find a balance between classes and a social life.

"I already told you I'm not going." I crossed my arms, hoping my body language would get my point across since my words were getting me nowhere.

"Come on, Allie. It's supposed to be the party of the semester. We can't miss it." Anne mirrored my pose. Probably trying to do the same thing—get her point across.

"What exactly makes something the party of the semester?" Tiffany asked. She was sitting on my bed reading *Mansfield Park*. Sometimes, watching Tiffany read the classics made me want to minor in English, but my recent decision to major in biochemistry instead of business was enough. The only good thing about being mad at my dad was that I didn't have to feel bad about not sticking with business.

"Good point." I smiled at Tiffany. "Besides, I never

said you guys can't go, but I don't feel like it."

"Is this just because of Nick?" Hailey turned in her desk chair.

"Yes, if I show up, he's going to get the wrong idea. There's no reason to encourage him." The party was at his Frat, and he'd made it a point to invite me—twice.

"Come on. Any guy who thinks he's got a shot at stealing you from Levi has to be crazy." Anne finally took a seat on the edge of Hailey's bed.

"Do you really care whether I go or not?"

"Yes! It's more fun when we all go together."

Hailey pushed her playfully. "In other words, she knows that Nick and his friends are going to give us all special treatment if you go."

"That's not true!" The look of horror that crossed Anne's face made it clear that's definitely not what she had in mind. "I just like hanging out with you."

"Fine. I'll go for a few hours."

"Awesome! Now we just have to find our outfits. It's a prohibition theme so we can wear those flapper dresses you wanted to wear for Halloween, Allie."

I laughed. Anne could be intense sometimes, but I loved her. In some ways, she reminded me of Jess, but I knew those similarities were really superficial. Both were so much more than the boy crazy shells they appeared to be on the outside.

"I guess we can. I'm sorry to run, but I really need to get to the gym."

"That's fine. I'll fill you in later." Anne gave me a hug.

"Looking for these?" Hailey tossed me the headphones I'd been digging in my desk for.

"Thanks. See ya guys."

I waved before I headed out the door. I couldn't slack on my next session with Jared.

***

"You made it." Nick smiled when he noticed us. We'd just gotten drinks at the formal bar they had setup. When the bartender asked what I wanted, my first thought was that I wished Levi was there to order my drink. I really needed to find out what it was.

"Yeah, I guess I did."

"You guess?" He smiled.

I shrugged. "Yeah..."

"I'd offer you a drink but you already have one."

"Yup." I held up the red plastic cup.

"I'm really glad you came. It's nice to see you outside of lab."

"Yeah, in the real world."

"Exactly. You look great, by the way."

I looked down at my black flapper dress. Leave it to Anne to find us all vintage dresses at the Salvation Army. "Thanks. You look the part, too."

"Oh, yeah. Cool." He adjusted the brim of his hat.

"Hey, Allie, I need your help with something." Hailey put a hand on my arm.

"Okay, no problem. Sorry Nick, but I need to help my friend."

"Oh, that's cool. I'll catch up with you later." He tried to play it off, but he was disappointed.

"The real world? Where'd you come up with that line?"

"Hey, I was grasping at straws. The guy's my lab partner. I'd rather not have to make things more awkward than necessary."

"He's already done that for himself."

I turned away to watch the Jazz Trio. I knew these parties could be cool, but I didn't expect actual live music. Between the bar, music, and the costumes, it was a pretty fun atmosphere. I enjoyed the music, and when I finished my second drink, I decided not to get another.

I was ready to go home. "You guys want to go?"

"Definitely... but where's Tiffany?" Hailey glanced around.

"I don't know…" I surveyed the room. "The last time I saw her she was talking to some guy with a blue tie and matching fedora."

We walked all over the house and yard but couldn't find her. I saw Nick and decided he could be of help.

"There you are. I've been looking for you." He grinned, taking my hand to pull me close to him. I smelled his breath—he reeked of alcohol.

"Have you seen my friend Tiffany? She's the blonde I was with?"

"Maybe…was she the one talking to Carl earlier?"

"She was talking to someone."

"Blue hat?"

"Yes."

"I think they went upstairs."

"Upstairs?" I was sure I hadn't heard him right.

"Yeah, it's off limits at parties unless you're with one of the brothers."

There was no way Tiffany would go up to some guy's room like that. Unless she was more drunk than I thought. "I have to find her."

"Want me to help you?"

"Could you?"

"Absolutely, come on." He took my hand again, pulling me through the crowd. Hailey and Anne trailed after us.

When we reached the staircase, he turned to my friends. "Sorry, just Allie."

"Is that a joke?" Hailey asked.

"No."

Hailey glared at him. "Why not? Afraid your brothers won't believe you can handle three girls?"

Nick choked on his beer.

"Let's go." Hailey pushed past him.

He took a step forward, placing a hand on her shoulder. "Hey, I told Allie I'd take her up, and my brothers know I could handle it, but she's the only one I want."

"Good luck with that." Hailey easily brushed off his hand, and continued up.

We followed behind.

A guy with short, black hair blocked Hailey at the top of the stairs.

"Where's Carl's room?"

"Carl's room? I think he's already busy, but I'm free, definitely free." He grinned at her.

"Does Carl happen to be busy with a blonde?"

"Maybe, why do you ask? I happen to love redheads."

"Okay, this is how it's going to work. You tell me where Carl's room is now, or I kick your ass."

He didn't have a chance to respond. Even with the blaring music, the unmistakable sound of screaming pierced through the air.

"What the fuck was that?" Nick asked, looking below us.

"I don't know, but I have to find Tiffany." My body and common sense were yelling at me to turn around and get the heck out of the house, but there was no way I was leaving Tiffany behind.

"Fine, I told you I'd help." Nick's expression revealed genuine concern. "Come on, Sean, they're looking for their friend."

"I'm sure she's fine. Carl's probably taking good care of her."

"Shut the hell up and help us find her." Anne put a hand on his chest. Hailey and I both looked at each other. Anne had more nerve than we expected.

Sean gave in, holding his hands up in front of himself in defeat.

We had just pushed our way past the guys when I heard the whoosh.

I turned around just in time to watch a wave of fire engulf the stairs.

"Shit, we have to get out of here," Nick yelled.

"How? We can't go back down those stairs." Sean

glanced around him nervously.

"We're not leaving without Tiffany. Where is Carl's room?"

"Upstairs," Nick finally answered. He was definitely starting to panic.

"There's another floor?" Anne asked.

"The stairs are down that hall, but we can't keep moving up. Let's go out a window."

"We're not leaving Tiffany," Hailey and I said at the same time.

Anne leaned over wheezing.

"Anne? Are you okay?"

She shook her head.

"Do you have your inhaler?" Anne had asthma that was usually well controlled.

She shook her head again.

"Let's find Tiffany and go." I moved toward the stairs without checking to see if the guys were following us. I felt the heat as the fire continued to spread across the floor boards. Smoke gradually filled the small hallway, and I fell to the floor. I crawled towards the wall. Anne was wheezing so hard, I knew she probably couldn't breathe.

I shook Hailey. "You have to get her out of here."

"I can't leave you and Tiffany."

"You have to. Hopefully she won't remember your wings. Come back for Tiffany and me, or get Levi."

"Allie, I can't."

"Do it, Hailey. Do it."

She nodded. "I'll be right back." She pushed open a door into a bedroom. I followed with Nick and Sean behind me. Hailey picked up Anne and jumped out. Her wings came out and she disappeared into the night.

"This smoke is making me hallucinate," Nick said to himself.

Sean looked out the window. "We have to jump. There's no other choice."

I stuck my head out the window and breathed in some

fresh air before heading back into the hallway. "I have to find her."

I didn't look behind me as I reached the hallway. The heat was intense, and I could barely see through the smoke. I looked toward the entryway to the second flight of stairs but it was blocked by a large piece of wood. Objects fell from the ceiling as the house appeared to be caving in. More screams could be heard from downstairs. I turned around and saw Nick trapped under fallen debris.

I crouched low and moved toward him. I tried to pull the boards off him, but they wouldn't budge.

"Nick, are you okay?" I asked, praying he'd respond. I coughed, the smoke was getting worse.

I saw the flames and knew it was over. I was going to die in a frat house fire. I didn't cry. I just wished I'd been able to see my family and Levi one last time.

The smoke was too much. I lay down, trying to cover my face with my hands. There was nowhere to go.

"I've got you, Al. I've got you." Through the haze, I heard his voice.

"Levi?" I choked out. I opened my eyes, feeling his strong arms around me.

"I've got you."

I looked around me. "But Tiffany and Nick."

"Jared has Tiffany. And who's Nick?"

"The guy over there." I didn't have the strength to point, but I knew he'd figure it out.

"We don't have time."

"Levi! Get him now or I won't ever talk to or look at you again."

"Fine." He adjusted me so I was in one arm and then moved the debris like it was nothing. He picked up Nick like a ragdoll and carried us into the bedroom where Hailey had left. Sean was gone. He must have jumped too. As Levi jumped out, the deafening sound of sirens pierced my ears. Without warning, Levi dropped Nick, before landing a few blocks over in the shadows of a house.

"Levi!"

"You're lucky I even grabbed him. I can't get slowed down again. I need to get you away from here."

"Where is everyone?" I tried to steady myself in Levi's arms.

"Your friends are already at the hotel. We need to go. I need to make sure you're okay."

I knew the tears were forming, so I let him pull me closer. "I'm so sorry I wasn't there sooner. I'm so sorry."

"It's not your fault."

"This wasn't a random fire, Allie, trust me." He kissed my cheek. "Can you handle a longer flight? We need to get downtown."

"Yes." I could still feel the heat across my body and the smoke in my lungs, but I wanted to get away. I needed to make sure my friends were okay.

Levi wrapped his arms around me and took off.

CHAPTER FOURTEEN

Levi landed on my balcony at the hotel. "We need to get downstairs, but Dr. Ellis is already waiting for us here."

He pushed open the door and carried me inside. Sure enough, the doctor was sitting on the couch. Helen sat next to him. I didn't bother to ask how they got in.

"Allie, oh my goodness." Helen moved to give me space on the couch. She took my hand.

"I'm fine," I assured her.

"We just need to make sure."

Dr. Ellis listened carefully with his stethoscope to my lungs. He then used a small penlight to look in my mouth, and he closely examined my skin.

"Are there any burns, other than the redness on your legs?"

"No. Nothing."

Dr. Ellis turned to Levi. "She's likely fine. She's very lucky you got to her when you did." He turned back to me. "Just keep the area clean and apply this antibiotic ointment daily." He handed me a tube.

"Thank you." This was the second time the doctor had examined me. I hoped it was his last. I liked him, but I was tired of getting hurt.

"Where's everyone else? Hailey, Anne, Tiffany?"

Helen squeezed my hand. "Tiffany's in the hospital. She was unconscious when Jared found her, but she's going to be okay."

"Oh my god. Is she alone?"

"Of course not. Hailey's with her. Her parents are already on their way."

I started to get up. "I need to see her."

Levi placed a hand on my shoulder. "You have to stay here."

"No. I'm okay."

"You need to rest. Besides, it's safer here. We need to keep you safe." His voice was soft, but there was an urgency in it.

"Safe? I am safe—you saved me."

Levi swallowed nervously. "I already told you this wasn't random."

"What aren't you telling me?"

He looked away from me. "You were the target."

My chest tightened. "What? How? Why?"

"We think it was Martin and his men, but we don't know for sure yet. I'll know more once we get downstairs."

"Then let's go." I hopped off the couch but moved so fast that I felt dizzy.

Levi caught me before I could fall. "Slow it down."

"We should go. You can get cleaned up downstairs." Helen looked at me sympathetically.

I nodded, not sure how I could get cleaned up in the basement. I didn't care. I needed more information.

"Is Anne there?" I realized no one had mentioned her.

"Yes. Hailey made sure she was okay before going to the hospital. I believe Anne's with Owen." Helen touched my arm gently before opening the door.

Levi insisted on carrying me all the way downstairs. He wouldn't even put me down in the elevator. I didn't complain—I was still shaken up. My chest clenched a little again as we entered the complete darkness of the basement.

***

"I'm not high, am I?" Anne asked as soon as she saw me. Levi set me down on a chair in some sort of sitting room in the basement.

I gave her a small smile. "No. You're not high."

"So you guys are actually half birds?"

"I already told you, Allie's human," Owen said in an exasperated tone I'd never heard him use before.

"Oh, excuse me. You guys, besides Allie."

Levi laughed. "Are you okay here? I need to find my dad."

I moved to get up. "I'm coming. You promised me answers."

"You'll get them, but right now you need to wait here. Please, Al, don't fight me just this once." Something in the way he pleaded kept me quiet. I nodded. He kissed me lightly on the forehead before leaving the room. Owen went with him.

Anne waited until the door clicked closed to start with more questions. "You knew what he was, right? When were you going to fill me in?"

"I knew, but—" I stopped, wondering how much I should tell her.

"Don't hold back on me now. Your roommate had wings grow out of her back. You might as well tell me the rest."

I smiled despite the somber mood of the evening. "When Owen told you I was human, did he tell you anything else?"

"He said you were Levi's mate. That's what I don't get. Why would you be his mate if you're human and he's not? And by the way, who is he? People were treating me like royalty when Owen told them I was your friend."

"Pterons usually go for humans, and Levi's a prince."

"A prince? You're the mate of a paranormal prince? So does that make you a princess?" she asked excitedly.

"So, you're no longer questioning your soberness?"

"No. But what were you about to tell me before?" She froze like a light bulb had gone off. "Wait, did you somehow not know what you were getting yourself into?"

"Not really." I looked away. "I didn't know I'd become his lifelong mate."

"Wow, it all makes sense."

"What makes sense?"

"Why you didn't want a guy that gorgeous calling you his fiancé. But how did he do it so that you didn't know what was happening? Drugs?"

"Sex."

Her eyes widened. "What?"

"He gave me a ring, and we had sex."

"Seriously?" She leaned forward in her seat.

I nodded. "Yes."

"That's pretty awesome."

"Awesome?" I asked incredulously.

"He's a paranormal prince. You do realize how cool that is, right?"

I laughed without meaning to, but once it started I couldn't stop. Anne joined in.

"So he's been trying to make it up to you, huh? Trying to get you to forgive him?" She crossed her legs, getting comfortable. She was eating it up.

I shifted uncomfortably. "Pretty much."

"So he can only have one mate?"

"Unfortunately."

"Please tell me you don't mean that."

I didn't know if I did or not. I shrugged.

"You're lucky. You've got a hot, powerful, rich guy wrapped around your finger. Embrace it."

"But I don't know how I can trust him."

"I didn't say to make it easy on him. Have you been with him since?"

"As in, have I slept with him again?"

"Yeah."

"No."

"That's good. You still have the power. Enjoy it—but not for too long. You might as well enjoy the rest of him too."

"That's one way to view it."

"Come on, Allie. You are obviously crazy in love with him." She picked up a throw pillow.

"Obviously?"

"Yeah. The way you look at him; the way you move around him, it's hard to miss."

"Oh."

"So, how does Hailey fit in?"

"She's Owen's sister."

"Which means…" Anne tied her hair up in a messy bun.

"Owen's one of Levi's best friends."

"So they're not royal?"

"No. But really, I don't get the hierarchy yet."

"You better learn it. You are the princess, after all."

I crossed my arms over my chest. It was always so cold down there, and my dress wasn't cutting it. "You're not going to let that go, are you?"

"Probably not." Anne got serious all of a sudden. "Tiffany's going to be okay, right?"

"I think so…that was crazy."

"No one's told me anything, and by the sound of it, they haven't told you either. What do you think happened?"

"They think another Pteron did it. Maybe to get to me…"

"Oh, that explains why they want us here."

"I hope we get to go home tonight, but we can always stay in my room upstairs if we need to."

"I'd rather not get burned to death, so I'll do what they say. Besides, I wouldn't mind spending some more time with Owen…don't tell Hailey, but he's pretty hot." Anne smiled.

"I *definitely* won't tell Hailey."

The door opened, and Owen walked in. His ears must have been ringing. "Levi wants me to take you to your room, Allie."

"Then why did he make me come down here to begin with?"

"Not that room. You have a room downstairs. It's a safe room."

"A safe room? Are you crazy? We can go upstairs."

"Anne can, but there are some extra beds down here if she'd prefer." He paused and looked at her.

"I'll take a guest bed downstairs. It seems safer."

"Okay, let's set Anne up and then we can continue discussing this, Allie."

"Fine." I understood why Anne wanted the room. The truth was, I was terrified too. "Can't I stay with Anne?"

"I don't think so. The king agreed you needed to be in your safe room."

"My safe room? What makes it mine?"

"It's Levi's…"

"Oh…"

"Yeah. The king has one, and the prince. It's always been that way."

We followed Owen down the hall, turned a few times and stopped in front of a door. He pushed it open, revealing two twin beds.

Anne eyed it approvingly. "Wow, nice guest digs."

Owen stepped back to let Anne move into the room. "Glad you like it. I bet Hailey will crash with you."

"Cool. Thanks." Anne smiled. She was taking things so well. I wondered when reality was going to set in. "Night, Allie. And by the way, you officially have my permission to enjoy all of him tonight if you're feeling up to it."

"Your permission? I don't think so. Goodnight, Anne."

"Night." She closed the door.

Owen raised an eyebrow. "Enjoy all of him?"

"Don't start."

He laughed. "I won't."

I followed him as he led me through two sets of double doors, each guarded by large guys I didn't recognize. I didn't need to ask to know they were Pterons.

Owen opened a metal door, and I entered Levi's safe room. "My bet is that this is fancier than the President's bunker."

Owen chuckled. "Yeah, I'd think so too."

The place was decorated to the nines with red tapestries. Marble floors matched the hallway, but the large bed in the center of the room was perched on a plush red rug. A crystal chandelier hung from the ceiling above the bed. A full dining set was positioned on the other side of the room, with a kitchen located off it.

"Is the bathroom just as nice?"

"I don't know, but I wouldn't be surprised."

"Great, I hope I can find something of Levi's to wear." I needed to get out of my ripped and dirty dress. I opened one of the large armoires stocked full of men's clothes.

I opened the armoire next to it, expecting to find more of the same, but it was full of women's clothing—all in my size.

"Please tell me Levi didn't buy all of this…" I closed a drawer after realizing it was full of lingerie.

"I would guess Helen did. This might be a safe room, but the Laurent's have been known to use their room for other reasons."

"Other reasons?"

He raised an eyebrow. "Can you get more privacy?"

"Ugh. We don't need to use ours for that reason."

He laughed again. "Weren't you supposed to be enjoying all of him tonight?"

I hit him on the arm. "Shut up."

"I'll get out of your hair then."

"Do that, and do me a favor and tell Levi I expect a full report."

"Aye, aye," he said in mock salute.

Owen left, and I jumped when I heard the door slam closed behind him. The room was completely silent once the door closed, and I couldn't help but feel trapped. As I looked around, I realized there could be much worse places to be confined.

I walked into the bathroom, and I'd been right—the place was gorgeous. There was a dual vanity with marble counters, a large soaking tub, and a shower big enough for two. I could have moved in.

I turned on the water in the shower, letting the whole bathroom get steamy before stripping off my dirty dress and stepping in. I hadn't thought to search for shampoo or soap or anything, but someone already had the shower stocked—with my favorites.

Under the hot water, the reality of how close I'd come to dying hit me. I started to shake, and I leaned against the shower wall to steady myself.

"Al? You okay?"

My heart jumped out of my chest even though I knew it was Levi.

"What are you doing in here?" I called after turning off the water.

"Owen said you wanted to talk."

"I do."

"Should I come join you, or do you want to do it out here?"

"Hand me a towel, Levi."

"If you insist." He tossed a towel over the top of the shower. I used the plush, red towel to dry off and squeezed some water out of my hair before wrapping up in the towel and stepping out.

Levi leaned against the vanity watching me. "I'd pay you a thousand dollars to drop that towel right now."

"Only a thousand? I thought I'd be worth more."

"Oh, you're priceless, love. I was just talking about a peek. I already know how gorgeous your body is, but I wouldn't mind a refresher image to work from."

"To work from?"

He grinned wickedly.

"Ugh."

"Would you rather I think about someone else? You haven't exactly left me with any choice."

"Your fault, not mine."

"But you're the one who can do something about that." His hands clenched the countertop like he was afraid that if he let go he wouldn't be able to control himself.

"It's not like I don't want you too." I regretted the words as soon as they left my mouth.

"Then drop the towel, Al. I promise I'll make it well worth your while."

I pulled the towel tighter around me. "Can you please keep your mind off sex for a minute? I almost died, and one of my best friends is in the hospital. I'm going to find something to wear." I didn't need to turn around to know he was following.

"How about these?" he asked, picking out a pair of red, lacy panties.

"Didn't your mom buy all of this?" I hoped the mention of his mom would cool things off.

"Not the stuff in this drawer." I tensed, as I felt his lips on my neck.

"Levi."

"Shh."

I closed my eyes, enjoying the feeling of his lips more than I should have. I opened my eyes and pulled away. "So that means there's more appropriate stuff in another drawer." I looked in the next drawer, pulling out a more practical pink pair. I also found a cami and shorts PJ set.

"You're going to wear these for me one day." He picked up the lacy pair again. He came closer, his lips inches from mine. "Just so I can take them off of you."

I shivered. "So I'm going to go change." I hurried back to the bathroom before he could tempt me anymore.

Dressed, I walked out of the bathroom, not surprised to see Levi reclining on the bed. He was wearing only a pair of boxers. I made my gaze return to his face. He caught where I'd been looking and grinned. "It looks like I'm not the only one looking for a refresher. I could remove the shorts if you'd like."

I ignored his comment. "Why aren't there couches in here? Why bother with the dining table and chairs, but nothing more comfortable?"

"What could be more comfortable than a bed?"

"Fine." I sat down cross-legged next to him. "Talk."

"You ordering me around now?"

"Yes."

"Okay then." He shifted, putting his hands behind his head. "It was Martin. We're sure of it."

"How are you so sure?"

"A scout saw him leaving right before the fire, and they found some other evidence at his apartment."

"So now what?"

"We keep you safe until we catch him. It won't be long. Jett Florence is already on his trail."

I shifted, moving further onto the bed. "You don't expect me to stay here until then, do you? I need to see Tiffany."

"Of course, you're staying. Tiffany is fine. They'll probably be sending her home tomorrow."

I was glad she was okay, but that didn't help the guilt. I thought staying in New Orleans would protect the people I loved, but all it did was endanger others.

I tried to push those thoughts away so I could focus on the present situation. "Where are you going to sleep?"

"Right here." He patted the bed beside him.

"I thought I was sleeping here."

"You are. We aren't supposed to need separate beds."

"You really think I'm going to sleep in the same bed as you?"

"We slept together after the meeting."

"On the couch."

"What's the difference? We'll just be more comfortable this way. It's convenient there's no couch, isn't it?"

"Convenient? Wait a minute."

I hopped off of the bed, and walked over to a space on the other side of the room with another plush rug. I bent down and, sure enough, there were some barely visible marks from where a sofa had recently stood. "You have to be kidding. You had the couch removed, didn't you?"

He smiled and shrugged. "It may have needed cleaning."

"Cleaning? When was it last used?"

"I sat on it once or twice, I think."

"You're unbelievable."

"I know." He smirked.

"That's not a compliment. And you're sleeping on the floor."

He shook his head. "No way."

"You could have had the couch, but you moved it."

"No." He actually looked flustered.

I crossed my arms. "Then I'm leaving."

"You go and try it."

I walked over to the door and tried to pull it open. It wouldn't budge. I knocked on it, but no one answered.

"We're locked in until morning, love. Security precaution."

"What if there is an emergency?"

"Theoretically, I might have the strength to get us out…"

"Then do it."

"I'm too tired. That fire exhausted me." He moved so he could throw back the covers and slip in. "You ready for bed?"

"Get out of that bed!"

"I'm too tired. Do me a favor and turn off your lamp when you decide to join me."

"Arrgh." I marched into the bathroom and slammed the door. When I came out, he was still in bed. I went over and shook him, he pretended to sleep.

"Get out!"

There was no way I was sleeping on the floor. That was his job. With a sigh of frustration, I climbed into the bed and turned off the light.

As soon as I laid down, his arms came around me.

"I thought you were sleeping."

"Your proximity woke me up."

"You better behave yourself." I wished I meant it.

"What does behaving myself involve?" he whispered.

"You understood the other night."

"But that was the couch, this is a bed. You've already explained how they're inherently different."

"Are you trying to annoy me?"

"No, I'm trying to seduce you, but whatever works."

"Seduce me? There are far better ways to do that."

"Are there? I'm listening." He brushed his lips against my cheek.

"Try being sweet and romantic."

"Doesn't locking you in a soundproof room count as romantic?"

"No."

"Darn, I knew I should have popped open some champagne."

"Champagne? You actually have that?"

"No, *I* don't, but *we* do. This is our room, sweetheart. Maybe we can open some tomorrow night."

"Tomorrow night? I'm going to need it if I'm locked in here with you again."

"You will be if we don't catch Martin. It's the safest way."

"You'll tell me the truth, right? If you catch him?"

"What are you suggesting?" He slipped a hand under

my tank, running his fingers over my stomach. "Are you implying I'd willingly mislead you in order to get you in bed again?"

"That's exactly what I'm suggesting."

"Then it's a good thing you admitted to wanting me too."

I pushed his hand away, and smoothed down my top. "It's not happening."

"Come on, you're not fooling me."

"What are you talking about?"

"You know I can see you perfectly, right?"

I guess I was more obvious than I thought.

"Good night, Levi." I rolled over.

"I'm not ready to say goodnight." He moved behind me, his arms wrapped around my waist.

"You were ready to fall asleep earlier."

"You woke me up."

He was close enough to me that I knew exactly what he meant. "It's not happening," I repeated.

"What can I do to change your mind?"

"Nothing. Go to sleep."

"You're no fun."

"I guess not." I closed my eyes, hating how much my body warred with me to turn around.

"Fine, but we're at least sleeping comfortably."

"This isn't comfortable?"

"It is, but I like this better." He moved onto his back, positioning me so that I was leaning my head on his chest. He pulled my arm over him. "I like to sleep on my back, and I like your head leaning on me. You comfortable?"

"Yeah," I admitted. "I'm good."

"Goodnight, Al." He used his other hand to run his fingers over the bare skin of my back that was revealed by my tank.

"Good night."

I had just about fallen asleep when I heard him whisper, "I love you."

"I love you, too," I whispered so softly that even with his super hearing he couldn't hear—at least I didn't think so.

CHAPTER FIFTEEN

Levi wasn't in bed when I woke up. I touched the empty space next to me, shocked he'd leave me alone. I got up and dug out more clothing from the armoire— settling on a t-shirt and jeans. I definitely wasn't putting on my ripped flapper dress. I grabbed a pile of clothes in case Hailey and Anne needed them too. I peeked into the bathroom, but Levi wasn't there either.

I banged on the door, hoping someone would open up. I didn't hear anything. "Hello? Is anyone out there?"

I didn't get a response, and I felt my frustration rising. I wasn't okay with being locked in a room anymore. I banged again. "Hello?"

I was just about to freak out when the door swung open. I expected Levi to be standing on the other side— but it was Bryant.

"Hello, Princess." It was exactly what Jared called me, but the way Bryant said it sounded different, more demeaning. Maybe it was also because he seemed so much older, especially wearing a dress shirt and slacks. I felt like a kid next to him.

"Hi, Bryant. Where's Levi?" I regretted my decision to

keep Bryant's behavior from Levi.

"He's with the king. I'm supposed to take you home."

"Are Owen and Jared busy?" Levi rarely trusted me with anyone but them.

"Yeah, they're busy."

"Okay. Have you seen my friends?"

He nodded. "They already left."

"Hailey and Anne left?"

"Uh huh, they left hours ago."

"Oh. Well, I'm sure I can just get myself home then. Or I can wait for Levi." I took a step back.

"He's going to be awhile."

I didn't particularly want to get a ride from Bryant, but I was definitely ready to get out of there. I wanted to see my friends, and I needed to check on Tiffany. "Have you heard any more about my friend who got hurt?"

"I heard she's fine. She looked worse than she was."

"Okay good."

"You ready?"

"Sure." I followed him out of the room.

We passed a few people I didn't recognize as we headed to the elevator. I tried to ignore the wave of disappointment I felt when I didn't see Levi as we headed out of the lobby and onto the street.

I got into the passenger seat of Bryant's gray Lexus.

"How did you get roped into taking me?" I fished out a stick of Chap Stick from my purse. I still couldn't believe it had survived the fire.

"I volunteered."

"You volunteered to babysit?"

He grinned. "Babysitting implies watching a kid. You're no kid."

"Still, I figure there would be other jobs you'd rather be doing. Aren't you supposed to be looking for Martin?" That's when it hit me. Why would Levi be okay with me leaving if Martin was still out there. "Wait, did you guys catch him?"

Bryant pulled out onto the road. "He's taken care of."

"Wow, that was fast."

Bryant laughed. "We're good at our job. You're in good hands." He put his hand on the back of my seat.

"Have you heard anything about the fire? Was anyone hurt? You said Tiffany is okay, but what about everyone else?" I wondered how Nick was doing after Levi dropped him like a sack of potatoes.

"No one died, if that's what you're asking." He said it nonchalantly but the very thought that someone could have died made me sick.

"I still don't understand why Martin did it. Aren't there easier ways to get at me?"

"Yes, much easier ones."

Clearly he wasn't trying to put me at ease. "Then why burn down a frat house?"

Bryant turned to look at me. "Martin's a little bit dramatic sometimes."

"It sounds like you know him well."

"I do. We were best friends growing up." He moved his right hand back to the wheel.

"Oh. I had no idea." The Pteron social circle could make a good soap opera.

"It's not something I advertise. He's had it out for Levi and his father for years."

"Why? Is he jealous or something?" I blatantly tried to comb out my hair with my fingers. I'd been in such a rush to get out that I hadn't even bothered to fix it. I quickly gave up and tied it back with an elastic.

Bryant kept his eyes glued on the road. "Or something."

"Are you going a different way? Wasn't that our turn?" I peered out the window.

"We're not going to Tulane, Allie."

"But you said you were taking me home."

"I'd think you'd be used to being lied to by now."

My stomach lurched. "Okay, what's going on? Does

Levi know I'm with you?"

"No, he doesn't know." His voice was as cold as ice.

"Then where are we going?" I grabbed the door latch with my right hand. My left hand moved to my seat belt.

Bryant grabbed my left wrist. "You can relax. You're not going anywhere."

"Why not?"

"Because I said so."

I struggled but his grip was too tight.

He pulled to a stop in the loading dock area of an abandoned warehouse. I glanced around for someone—anyone. Surely it couldn't be that desolate in the middle of the morning.

"We're going to make this easy. Don't fight me and you might live through it." He pulled me over the console and out his door. His grip was so tight, I knew I'd have bruises. He pulled me inside the warehouse and moved over a chair to block the door.

I tried to appear more in control of my nerves than I actually was. "What do you want from me?"

"Now that's an interesting question." His eyes raked over me.

"I doubt you went through all of this effort just to get some."

"No. I didn't actually, but if that's a side benefit, I'll take it."

I needed to stall whatever plan he had. "Does this have to do with the Blackwells?"

"Of course, it does."

"So you're going to turn me over to them?"

"Maybe, maybe not." He held up his hands like a scale.

"What do you mean?"

"My job was to get you away from Levi. Where we keep you is up to me."

As I listened, I tried to formulate a plan. There was no way I was getting locked up by some crazy Pterons for the rest of my life. Being kidnapped by Cougars was bad enough. I couldn't believe I was going through it again.

"What are the options?"

"That depends on you."

"How so?"

"I see the way you look at me. You want me as much as I want you."

My first impulse was to argue, but I realized that wouldn't help. I had to somehow convince him he was right. "So? I'm sure lots of girls are attracted to you."

He smiled. "True, but none like you."

"Do you usually flatter your kidnap victims?"

"How many girls do you think I've kidnapped before?"

"Lots."

"Nope, you're the first."

"You're supposed to be giving me my options." I tried to make myself sound flirtatious.

"Oh yes, how could I forget?" He took a step towards me. "I can hand you over to the Blackwells and let them do what they please, or…"

"What?"

"You can stay with me."

"Stay with you?"

"Yes. I think we'd have a good time together." He grinned impishly.

"You don't think Levi would find me?"

"Not a chance…you wouldn't want him to find you, would you?" He reached a hand out to stroke my cheek.

I forced a smile. "I choose option B."

"That quickly?"

"You already pointed out the obvious, Bryant. I want you."

"If that's true, then how about right here, right now." He pulled the elastic out of my hair, breaking it into two. His heated look terrified me. He wasn't someone whose advances I could fend off.

"You have to get me in the mood." God, if anyone could see me, I'd die. Maybe if all else failed, I could go into acting.

"My pleasure." He reached a hand out to touch me again, but I stopped him.

"Show me your wings."

"My wings?"

"Yeah. I kind of have a thing for them."

He grinned. "You really are meant to be with a Pteron. I'm guessing it's true what they say about certain humans being tailor made for us."

I ignored his comment, even though I wanted him to explain it. I had to keep things moving along.

I gave him the most flirtatious look I could muster. "Aren't you going to show me your wings now?"

He pulled off his t-shirt, tossing it to the ground. I took in a breath as I waited for his wings to appear behind him. Now came the tough part.

"Can I touch them?" I bit my lip. Maybe I was overdoing it, but he didn't seem to notice.

"Yeah, you can touch them. But then I get to touch you."

I smiled and moved closer to him. I reached behind him and ran my hand over one wing. "Nice."

"My turn."

"Not yet." I slowly moved around him until I was directly behind him. "I need the full effect." I knew I only had seconds. If he figured out what I was doing, I was as good as gone.

I put my hand on the exact spot Jared had shown me and pushed up.

"What the fuck?" He reached to move my hand but I pushed harder and held it. He cursed but didn't struggle. He couldn't move.

I pulled out my cell phone and dialed Levi. "I'm in the warehouse district, on Tchoupitoulas Street. It's directly across from some church. Come now."

"Are you okay? What happened?" He sounded panicked. He knew I was missing.

"Just get here *now*."

"On my way."

I hung up. I hoped the effect wouldn't wear off too soon. I had no plan B.

"They'll never believe you," Bryant snarled.

"Shut up." Levi would believe me. If I didn't trust in that, I was really in trouble.

Minutes later, the door barged open and Levi, Jared, and Jett Florence walked in.

"What the hell are you doing?" Jett moved toward me, but Levi and Jared were faster. Jared covered my hand with his, easing mine out so he could take over.

"He kidnapped me. He was going to give me to the Blackwells." I decided to leave out the other option he'd offered.

"Bullshit. The bitch is lying," Bryant snapped.

"I am not. Why else would I be here?"

"I never gave you permission to go near her. What the hell are you doing with her, Bryant?" Levi's eyes were solid black. He was ready to attack.

"Bryant, this has to be a misunderstanding. What's really happening?" Jett watched his son with a look of desperation.

"Other than the fact that Levi's mate was about to fuck me to avoid going to the Blackwells, not much has been happening."

Levi punched Bryant in the face. Blood oozed out of his nose.

I could taste bile. "You know it was an act. I had to get to your wings."

"How the hell did you learn to do that?" Bryant sneered.

I glanced at Jared. He nodded. "You needed that sooner than I expected."

"Are you really working with the Blackwells?" Jett had his head in his hands.

"Don't look so surprised."

Jett shook his head and made a call.

Evidently, punching Bryant had calmed Levi down, because he was suddenly at my side. "I'm sorry I let this happen. I thought you were still in the safe room."

"I just wish I hadn't been stupid enough to go with him."

"Why was it stupid? You knew he was Jared's brother."

"Yeah, but something felt off. You wouldn't have arranged for me to leave like that without saying goodbye."

"I'm glad you realize that, but there's no reason to feel stupid. But for future reference, no one but me, Owen, Jared, or Hailey is taking you anywhere."

"Did you really catch Martin?"

"Yes. We were interrogating him this morning. That's the only reason I left. I'd just discovered you were missing when you called."

Two men entered the warehouse. They bound Bryant, freeing Jared from his position at his back.

"What are they going to do with him?"

Levi ran his hand through my hair. He always found ways to touch me. "Interrogate him. We need to figure out what he was planning and how he ties to Martin. I thought they hadn't spoken in years, but this can't be a coincidence."

"Can we go home now?"

"Sure, but I want to stay with you for a while. You've been hurt way too much in twenty four hours."

"I wasn't hurt." Even as I said it, I rubbed my wrist.

Levi picked up my wrist and kissed it. Sometimes he surprised me with his sweet side.

"Nice job incapacitating him, by the way." He watched me intently.

"Don't get mad at Jared. It wasn't his fault."

Levi's lips curled up into a smile. "I knew."

"You knew?"

"You didn't really think I would have kept the truth from him, did you?" Jared appeared beside me.

"You acted like it. You made it sound like you were afraid of Levi finding out."

Levi held me tightly against his side. "I actually thought it was a good idea. I just didn't get why you didn't ask me."

"You're not mad, are you?"

"No. I'm just glad you asked someone who could teach you well."

"Yeah, he is a pretty good teacher."

Levi laced his fingers with mine. "Any chance I can take over the lessons now?"

I thought it over for a second. Maybe it was for the best. "Can you both train me?"

Levi laughed. "You're really serious about this, huh?"

"Considering what just happened, I don't see why you're laughing."

"You're amazing, Al. That's all." He ran a hand down my back.

"So what about taking me home?"

"Absolutely, but I'll have to borrow a car. I obviously flew." There was no other way they could have made it so fast.

"Take Bryant's car. He won't be needing it." Jared tossed a set of keys to Levi.

As much as I didn't want to get back in that car, I wanted to go home.

"All right, let's get out of here."

Chapter Sixteen

"Are you okay?" Hailey was waiting for me when Levi parked.

"Yeah, I'm fine." I tried to smile at her reassuringly.

She hugged me. "I'm so sorry I wasn't with you."

"Where were you, Hailey? Did you take Anne back?" Levi asked.

"Yes." Hailey avoided his eyes when she answered.

"Okay." Levi looked skeptical, but he didn't push it. "Let's get Allie upstairs."

"I'm fine. You can go."

"Not a chance. I already told you I'm staying for awhile. You might have a delayed shock." He put an arm around me as we walked toward my dorm.

"I'm not in shock. I think I'm starting to get used to getting kidnapped."

He stiffened. "That isn't funny."

"I wasn't joking." I didn't want to upset him, but the truth was that he put me in danger the moment he decided to give me the ring.

On Levi's insistence, we took the elevator. It was that or let him carry me upstairs. It was with relief that I collapsed on my bed. Levi nudged me over so he could lie next to me. At least he took his shoes off first.

"Ugh, I forget how uncomfortable these beds are."

"You don't have to sleep on it, so it's not an issue."

"You don't either." He touched my cheek.

"Yes I do." I sat up on an elbow so I could see Hailey over Levi. "How's Anne? Have you heard anything about Tiffany?"

"Anne's fine. She's taking it well."

"I'm actually not surprised."

Levi laughed. "You took it well too, Al."

"I guess I did…"

Hailey sat down on her bed. "And Tiffany is okay. They kept her overnight to check for inhalational burns, but everything came back clean. She really is lucky."

I felt sick just thinking about it. "Or unlucky for being my friend. She was only in danger because of me."

"That's not true." Levi turned to look at me.

"He's right. You can't start blaming yourself for everything," Hailey said softly.

"Easy for you to say." I yawned. I guess everything with Bryant made me tired.

"You can close your eyes. I'll be right here." Levi played with a strand of my hair.

"You really don't have to stay."

"I want to."

"Do you guys want privacy?" Hailey stood up, ready to leave the room.

"No, that's okay." I answered quickly. Levi nodded.

"If you're sure." Hailey sat down at her desk.

I fell asleep to the sound of her typing.

I woke up a few hours later tucked under my covers. Levi was gone. I sat up disoriented. Hailey was playing a game on her phone.

"What time is it?"

"Six."

"Six o'clock at night? You let me sleep all day?"

"You needed it."

I stretched. "When did Levi leave?"

"A few hours ago. He fell asleep too." She tossed me her phone. "Check out this picture. I already emailed it to you both."

I glanced at her phone. There was a picture of Levi and I snuggled up asleep. I had to admit it was cute. "You sent it to Levi?"

"I figured it would earn me brownie points. I have a feeling I'm in trouble." She leaned up against the wall.

"Why? Why are you in trouble?"

"I shouldn't have left the hotel without you. I should have waited."

"You took Anne home, and you thought I was safe. You can't be with me all the time."

"I should have come back after dropping Anne off, but I didn't." She bit her nail. I'd never seen Hailey do that before.

"Is there something you're not telling me?"

"This stays between us, okay?"

"Of course." I looked at her nervously. That opening was usually a bad thing.

"I got lunch with Cole."

"Cole? You mean the bouncer from Bruno's?" We'd run in to him a few times, and it was obvious he had a thing for Hailey.

"Yes." She still didn't meet my eye.

"Why is that a secret?"

"Remember what I told you about Pteron's dating?"

"You aren't supposed to get serious with anyone but a human."

"And you're definitely not supposed to date lower shifters…" She trailed off.

"Wait, what's Cole?" I'd always assumed he was a Pteron because he seemed part of the inner circle.

"He's a Grizzly."

"He's a bear?" I'd figured out that most shifter names

related to the type of animal they were.

"Yes. In terms of shifters he's high up, especially because his grandfather saved Levi's grandfather, but he's still below a Pteron."

"So that's why he had such a good seat at the meeting."

"Yes."

"I'm guessing that doesn't change the dating rules?"

She sighed. "No."

I crossed the room and sat next to her. "I'm sorry, Hail. You like him, huh?"

She evaded my question. "It's not a big deal. But it makes my screw up even worse. My parents are going to kill me."

"They won't find out."

"Yes they will."

"Give me a second."

"What?"

I picked up my phone and called Levi.

"Hey, how are you feeling, Sleeping Beauty?"

"You really like to call me princess names, don't you?"

He laughed. "Well, you are my princess."

"I guess that's true. The reason I'm calling is because of Hailey."

"What?" She stood up.

I waved Hailey off.

"She wasn't there because she was taking care of Anne, and making sure she wasn't going to tell everyone about The Society. Hailey should be rewarded for being so careful, don't you agree?" Levi was usually really good at reading me, so I hoped he understood what I was doing.

"Absolutely. I'll make sure her parents know." I could hear him smiling through the phone. He really could be a decent guy sometimes.

"Great, talk to you soon." I hung up.

"Now you can stop worrying."

She let out a deep breath. "You didn't have to do that."

"Want to make it up to me?"

"Yes, anything." She looked at me eagerly.

"Order us something good and greasy for dinner. I need it."

"I can definitely do that."

"Good." I loved my best friend.

***

I folded my laundry and took my time putting it away. As soon as I finished, I'd be out of excuses not to call my mom. She was going to kill me. Thanksgiving was just as big as Christmas to her. It was bad enough I'd stayed in New Orleans for school. Now I was canceling my first trip home.

I finally built up the nerve to call her. "Hey, Mom."

"Hey, honey. I haven't heard from you in a while. How've you been?"

"I'm doing fine, just busy with school."

"Have you decided when you're coming home?"

I swallowed. "I'm not coming, Mom."

She sighed into the phone. "What's going on?"

"Nothing. I just have too much work."

"You can get plenty of studying done here." I could hear the pleading in her voice.

"Not without distractions."

"Do you want us to come there?"

"Who's us?" I played with a feather that had come loose from my down comforter. It was overkill for New Orleans, but I loved the shade of blue.

"Steven, Andrew, and I."

I wasn't sure I'd ever get used to the idea that my mom was seriously dating the father of a guy I hated in high school. "No, it's okay. I'll see you in December anyway."

"We've never spent Thanksgiving apart." The disappointment in her voice hurt, but I didn't see any way around it. It had only been a few weeks since the fire, and although the buzz was finally dying out on campus, I wasn't over it. I couldn't believe that because of me, hundreds of people could have died, including a good friend.

"I'm sorry."

"If you weren't okay, you'd tell me, right?"

"Yes." I hated lying, but I didn't have any choice.

"You need to do what you need to do. You're an adult, and I can't force you to do anything anymore. If you change your mind, you know we'd love to have you."

"Thanks, Mom."

I wanted to go, but I couldn't. I didn't want to go home if it meant bringing guards with me, and taking the chance of endangering the people I loved. It was bad enough my friends were involved.

I hung up and tried to fight off the tears I knew were threatening to spill. I gave up the fight just as I heard a soft knock on the door.

"Are you okay?" Tiffany took a seat next to me on my bed.

"Yeah, sorry."

"Do you still want to go for manicures, or do you want to skip?"

"I want to go." I wiped my eyes.

"Is there anything you want to talk about?"

Tiffany had to be the nicest friend I'd ever had. I loved Hailey, and Anne was cool, but Tiffany was just so sweet.

"I had to tell my mom I wasn't going home for Thanksgiving."

Tiffany put a hand on my arm. "Oh, I'm sorry. That must have been rough. Are you sure you can't just ask Levi to go with you?"

"Theoretically, I could, but he's so busy with his dad right now, and honestly I don't think I'm ready to bring him home."

Some people might have pushed me, but Tiffany just smiled. "Well, at least you get to spend it with Hailey and Owen. That should be fun, right?"

"Definitely. I'm curious what a Pteron Thanksgiving is like." I loved that I didn't have to hide The Society from my friends anymore. Tiffany had taken it about as well as Anne. She said she always knew there was something different about the guys and Hailey.

"Speaking of Hailey, where is she? Isn't she coming with us?"

"Nope. She had to meet for a group project."

"Wait, so they're actually letting you out on your own?"

I laughed. "Yeah right. Let me out without a chaperone?"

"Then who's coming with us?"

"Jared."

The look of horror that crossed Tiffany's face was almost comical. "Jared's coming with us to get manicures?"

"Well, I doubt he's going to get his nails done. When Hailey cancelled, I had to find an alternative. Jared was more than happy to oblige when he found out you were coming."

Tiffany blushed. "Come on, that's not true."

"Yes it is. I don't know what happened the night of the fire, but he's been acting even weirder than usual ever since."

"I already told you, I don't remember what happened. I just remember feeling really dizzy and light-headed and the next thing I knew, I woke up in the hospital."

"I know. But I think Jared was scared he was too late."

"I can't believe I slept through a hot guy flying me to safety."

I laughed. "It was more than sleeping. But if you want to try flying, I'm sure Jared would oblige. But, I'd make him swear to be on good behavior."

"Sometimes I think this is all a dream. Like I fell asleep reading one of my Paranormal Romance's or something."

"Don't I know."

"Are you ready to go?"

I got up. "Sure. Jared's waiting."

Before we could walk out the door, my phone rang. I debated picking up when I saw my dad's name on the screen, but I was tired of fighting with him.

"Hi, Dad."

Tiffany gestured that she'd wait in her room.

"Hi, sweetie. I owe you an apology." His voice was soft, and I could tell he meant it.

"You do, but I understand."

"Everything is okay now."

"Really?" I asked with surprise.

"Yes. We got some new investors, and I think we can go ahead with the openings we had planned for next year." I could hear him smiling through the phone.

"Wow, that's great."

"Isn't it? These investors came out of nowhere, but they checked out."

"I'm glad to hear that."

"Are you spending Thanksgiving with your mom?"

It was rare enough to talk to one parent in a day, now I was talking to two. "Nope, I'm going to spend it with my roommate's family."

"Oh. This isn't because of your mother's boyfriend, is it?"

"No, not at all."

"Are you sure? I can fly back from China early if you want me to."

China? I had no idea he was in Asia. "No, I'm all set."

"Okay, just let me know if you change your mind."

"I will, but my friend is waiting for me. I love you, Dad."

"I love you, too. Have fun."

At least I was on speaking terms with both parents—hopefully it could stay that way for a while.

***

"The least I can do is help cook. It is my fault the royal family is coming." I washed my hands in the large farmhouse sink in the kitchen of Hailey's childhood home.

Jan laughed. "Are my nerves that obvious? I am honored they decided to come to my home for the holiday."

"I wouldn't say they were obvious, but if they were, it would be understandable."

It was the night before Thanksgiving and Hailey's mom was rushing to finish the rest of her preparations. I hadn't really considered that Levi would want to spend Thanksgiving with me, but he insisted on it. Originally, he wanted me to spend it at his house, but I'd already accepted Hailey's invitation. His solution was to invite himself, which also meant his parents.

Jan filled a large pot with water. "You wouldn't happen to know how to make cranberry sauce, would you?"

"You just add sugar with water and boil the cranberries, right?"

"That's pretty much it. The cranberries are in the fridge."

"I'll take care of it."

I was glad to be making myself useful. Hailey and Owen were out getting a few things at the store with their dad. I'd stayed back to help in the kitchen.

I found a saucepan, the cranberries, and some sugar, and went to work.

"I'm sure this isn't easy for you." Jan paused from cutting up vegetables.

I was sure that she wasn't talking about making cranberries. "What part?"

"Any of it. Hailey told me you were upset about missing Thanksgiving with your mother."

"I am, but I'll find a way to see her over the holiday break, hopefully."

"I'm sure she's missing you, too."

I just smiled and turned back to the stove.

Loud voices interrupted us as Hailey, Owen, and their father burst into the kitchen. "The store was a zoo. We're not going out again." Timothy paused in his rant to give his wife a kiss on the cheek.

Jan smacked him playfully with a dish towel. "That's good, because I can use you in here."

I finished up the cranberries. "Do you want me to wait for them to cool?"

"No, that's okay. Why don't you kids go relax. Thanks for the help, Allie." I'm pretty sure Jan felt bad accepting my help at all.

"It was no trouble."

It had actually been nice. I'd started to really appreciate the little things. I loved when I could forget about the craziness that was my life.

***

I'd never set a table for such a large number of people before. Compared to many Thanksgivings, it was small. Hailey's extended family lived a few hours away and did Thanksgiving with her grandparents. Still, most of the Thanksgivings of my childhood were just Mom, my grandparents, and I.

"Happy Thanksgiving, babe." Levi wrapped his arms around me from behind. I put down the last of the plates and turned to look at him. He'd slowly but surely started calling me babe again.

He'd stayed away from it ever since I screamed at him for calling me baby—too many bad memories. I decided the shortened babe form didn't bother me as much.

"Happy Thanksgiving." Levi looked great in a blue collared shirt and khaki slacks. We hadn't planned it, but we practically matched. I was wearing a blue sweater that was the same shade as his shirt.

He leaned down and kissed me lightly on the lips. I closed my eyes for a second, opening them to see Robert standing directly behind Levi with a grin.

"Oh, hello, Robert."

"Nice to see you, Allison."

I looked around for Helen, but she must have gone right into the kitchen to help Jan.

"Happy Thanksgiving," I said awkwardly.

"Maybe next year the two of you will host Thanksgiving?"

"Uh, maybe." I might have been able to make cranberry sauce, but any Thanksgiving I hosted would probably have to be ordered in.

"I should make sure they don't need help in the kitchen." I slipped out of Levi's arms and out of the room.

"Hi, Allie." Helen greeted me warmly. As I expected, she was in the kitchen trying to help Jan.

"Hi, Helen."

To Jan's credit, she wasn't showing any of the nerves.

We'd just sat down to eat when the doorbell rang.

"I'll get it." Hailey got up and went out to the front hall. I heard a muffled conversation, and then she walked back in, followed by Jared. He carried a bottle of wine.

"Is it too late to join you?"

"Of course not, Jared. You're always welcome here." Jan busied herself setting another place at the table. Jared took a seat next to Owen.

"How nice of you to join us." Robert turned his attention to Jared.

"Dad decided he didn't want to celebrate this year, but I didn't agree."

"He's taking Bryant's disloyalty hard." Robert took a sip of his wine. "That's to be expected."

"Of course he is. The perfect son did the unforgiveable. Now he's just left with me."

It was weird hearing Jared talk about himself so negatively. I wondered if he'd been drinking.

"You'll make him proud." Robert kept a stony expression, but behind his eyes I thought there was something else. I think he really cared about Jared.

Dinner was pleasant enough. I ate far too much and was more than happy to take a walk when Levi suggested it. We walked the few blocks to Audubon Park. After a few months in New Orleans, I'd decided the park was my favorite escape. In some ways, it was like an oasis in the city.

"I need to ask you something." Levi grabbed my hand, holding it tightly in his as we walked under the live oaks.

"Should I be worried?"

"No. It's a good thing."

I pulled my left sleeve down as far as it could go. It was probably sixty degrees, but I was cold. Levi got the hint, and put an arm around me. "I need to go on a business trip in a few weeks, and I want you to come with me."

"A business trip?" I stopped in front of one of the ponds.

"Yes. It's a few hours away, and it would be great if you could come. I promise we'll have fun."

"What happens if I say no?"

"Honestly? My dad will probably want to talk to you."

"Are you ever going to tell him?" I sat down on a bench watching some ducks play around in the water.

"There's no reason to. We're back together."

I turned to him. "Levi…"

"Just say you'll come."

"Is it at least someplace cool?"

"Define cool?"

I sighed. "Oh no."

"So you'll come?"

"Do I have a choice?"

He grinned. "No."

I'm sure I could have kept arguing, but the truth was, the thought of a few days away with Levi didn't sound nearly as bad as it might have a month before. "As long as I don't have to miss class."

"You won't."

"Okay."

He tightened his arms around me. "It's going to be fun."

"We'll see about that." I wasn't quite sure what I was agreeing to, but at least it would be a change of scenery.

"Can I ask you a question now?" Something had been bugging me since I talked to my dad.

He got up and pulled me to my feet so we could continue walking. "You can ask me anything."

"Remember how my dad was having all those business problems?"

He turned toward me. "Yes. I remember that well."

"Dad called and told me everything is fine because they have new investors. Did you have anything to do with that?"

"Did he say I did?"

"No. But it just seemed surprising that out of nowhere he'd have new ones."

"You're family, Al. That means I'm going to help." He walked ahead.

"Is that a yes?"

"Come to your own conclusion." He smiled.

"Thanks. His company means everything to him."

Levi looked at me seriously. "No, it doesn't. It can't mean everything, because he has you."

I leaned up and kissed Levi on the lips.

CHAPTER SEVENTEEN

"Remind me again why we had to take my car?" I cringed as Levi drove my Land Rover through another patch of mud. He had to run the windshield wipers to clean off enough mud for us to see.

"Because my car couldn't do this. It's what this car is meant for."

"So what would you have done if I didn't have a car that could?"

He downshifted. "I would have stayed on the main roads."

"Levi!"

"Relax, Al. I'll have your car looking as good as new."

"You think I'm only worried about my car?"

I grabbed the 'oh my god' bar, needing it more than ever as he drove through an area that shouldn't have been called a road. "I'm a little concerned about my life, too."

"Don't be." He looked over at me.

"Watch where you're driving!"

"My driving scares you more than my flying, doesn't it?"

"Maybe. Come on, please slow down."

"Only because you said please." He let off the gas a little.

I sighed. "How much further?"

"Another twenty minutes, maybe."

"Good."

He squeezed my hand. "I'm glad you're with me."

"At the moment, I'm regretting it."

"It's going to be fun."

"Fun? Isn't this a work trip?" I looked out the window at the endless trees. We were definitely in the middle of nowhere.

"Work is a relative term."

"How relative?" I stretched out my legs.

"Tonight's a dinner we can't miss, and tomorrow I have to preside over the dispute courts, but otherwise we're free."

"And what am I supposed to do while you're presiding over the court?"

"Sit and look pretty."

"That had better be a joke."

He laughed. "You're welcome to give me your opinion, but a lot of these issues are going to be new to you."

"Meaning they are paranormal?"

"Yup. It should be an eye opening experience." I was starting to think that everything surrounding The Society was eye opening. Nothing was straight forward.

"I bet," I grumbled. I didn't want to admit exactly how nervous I was. I'd agreed because I didn't think I had a choice, and in theory it sounded cool.

I closed my eyes and leaned back into the leather seat.

"I hope you're not worrying about your classes again."

I opened my eyes. "Of course, I am. Exams are next week."

"You're not even missing class. It's study period."

"Yes, study period. I'm supposed to be studying."

He touched my arm gently. "You're going to pass your tests, Al."

"I want to do more than pass."

"You'll be fine." He ran his fingers down my arm. Even over my long sleeve t-shirt, it felt good. "All right, we're just about there."

"Here? Where the hell are we?"

"Just outside Shreveport."

"It looks like the woods."

"It is the woods. Notice how I said just outside."

We pulled out of the trees, and Levi turned onto another dirt road. At least this one looked like someone had used it in the last fifty years. He parked the car in front of a rustic looking house.

"This is it?"

"It's where we're staying. It might not look like much on the outside, but the inside's nice." He got out and came around to open the door. "Come on."

I unbuckled, and took my backpack and purse. Levi already had our other bags.

He unlocked the front door, and I followed him in.

"Wow." I put down my stuff and walked around the open room. Exposed rafters went with the rustic look of the place, but plush couches, hardwood floors covered by several large area rugs, and a huge fireplace gave the room a really comfortable feel.

"I love this place. It's probably the smallest of our homes, but sometimes small is better."

"Smallest?"

"It's only one bedroom. Originally, there were two small ones, but Dad combined them."

"One bedroom?"

"Yes, love, one bedroom."

"So you're sure you can stand more time in bed with me without sex?"

"I think that's a question you should be asking yourself."

"I already know the answer, and at least there's a couch."

"Those couches aren't as comfortable as they look." He grinned.

"So are you going to show me this bedroom?"

"Of course." He took off down a narrow hallway and opened the door to a large room. Sparsely furnished, a king sized bed stood in the center of the room with bed stands and a dresser finishing off the space.

"Nice."

"Isn't it?" He crossed his arms, leaning against the bed post.

"What time is our dinner tonight?"

"It's at seven, so we have some time to explore if you want."

"Explore?"

"You brought your hiking shoes, right?"

I shook my head. "Umm, no. You never mentioned hiking."

"I'm sure you brought sneakers. That's all you need."

"Fine, give me a minute."

"Absolutely, I'm going to check out the wine selection. The caretaker should have stocked it, but I want to be sure."

"Wine? Won't alcohol be served at the dinner?"

"Yes, but I want to pick out something nice for tomorrow night."

"Tomorrow night?"

He smiled. "Yes, for when I make dinner for you."

"You're making me dinner?"

"Yes, and since you can't possibly have any other plans, you're not getting out of it."

"Okay…"

"Find your sneakers and do whatever you need to do, and then let's head out."

I dug out my sneakers from my bag and used the bathroom. I brushed my hair, pulling it back into a ponytail.

Levi was waiting for me in the kitchen. "You ready?"

"Sure, let's explore."

He grabbed my hand, towing me out the door.

We walked silently into the woods. I let him lead the way as we moved so far in that it got dark. "Are you sure you know where we're going?"

"Of course. This isn't my first time here."

"This might sound like a weird question, but where did you sleep when you came, since there was only one bedroom?"

He laughed. "I slept where we're sleeping."

"Then, where did your parents sleep?"

"The main house."

"So we're in…"

"The guest house. I just like it better."

"Oh…"

"When I was a kid I stayed with my parents, but I started staying in the guest house at sixteen or so. I'd drive out here to get away."

Every time I learned anything about Levi's childhood, it surprised me. He always seemed so polished. It was hard to imagine him as a teenager trying to escape his parents.

"I get that. I'm sure there was a lot of pressure."

"That's putting it mildly."

"This is a big deal, right?" I didn't take my eyes off the path in front of me. I was usually well coordinated, but coordination did nothing when it came to tree stumps.

"Presiding?"

"Yeah."

"Very. Dad letting me take over a session means he's testing me, seeing if I'm ready for more. If this one goes well, he'll hopefully let us do some in cooler places."

"You say that, but you like it here."

He smiled. "Yeah, but I wouldn't mind seeing other places with you…"

He stopped walking and put his hands on my waist. "There are so many places I want to take you."

"What places?"

"All over the world…but most of our travel will be in North and South America—our territory."

"So someone else runs the other continents?"

"Yeah. My dad's second or third cousins or something run Europe, and I've met the family in Africa, but I don't know much about the others. It's hard enough to deal with all of the families in our territory."

"Like the Blackwells…"

He leaned in closer. "You don't need to worry about them, Al. You know I'm going to keep you safe."

"I know." I tried not to think about how close I'd come to getting held hostage by them or worse just a few weeks before. I knew it wasn't Levi's fault, but it definitely made me doubt my safety—at least when I wasn't with him. Somehow, being tucked in Levi's arms made me feel like nothing could ever hurt me. I might have gotten annoyed at Levi a lot, but I didn't doubt his strength or devotion to protecting me.

He leaned down and kissed me gently on the lips. "Do you want to keep going?"

"Sure, I'm not usually a woodsy person, but this is pretty cool."

"Want to fly a little? There's somewhere I want to show you."

"Do you even have to ask?" I doubted I'd ever get tired of flying. It was a high like no other.

"I guess not."

Seconds later, we were airborne. The trees moved under us in a blur. I quickly stopped looking at them. It was easier to just look straight ahead. Levi landed on the rocky shore of a river.

I understood why Levi liked the spot. It was straight out of a postcard. The river rushed by quickly, the running water the only sound other than the occasional bird chirping.

"This is beautiful."

"It's one of my favorite spots." He sat down on a rock,

making room for me next to him.

"You have favorite spots that don't serve alcohol?"

"Low blow."

"Just saying."

"I happen to like 'woodsy' stuff." He made air quotes as he said woodsy.

"You can't blame me for my lack of exposure to the outdoors. My dad didn't exactly take me camping growing up."

"Is it something you'd want to do?"

"Go camping?"

"Yeah. I promise, I'd go easy on you. We wouldn't have to rough it too much."

I wasn't sure how I felt about this side of Levi—it was so different. Where was the teasing guy who always dressed impeccably, and picked out the fancy wine? It's like being out in the woods had changed him.

"Maybe."

"I'll take a maybe."

We sat watching the river for a while. After a half hour, he actually managed to teach me to skip rocks. Granted, I could only get one or two skips, where as he could get twice as many.

My stomach rumbled.

He turned to me. "All right, let's get back."

"Do we have to?" I smiled at him. Maybe he wasn't the only one who loved being in the middle of nowhere. It was nice to escape from everything else. I realized I hadn't even brought my phone on the hike. It was the farthest from the device I'd willingly been in years.

"We can come back tomorrow, if you want."

"You promise?"

"I promise." He stood up, giving me a hand to help me up.

"Thanks for this."

"My pleasure. It's nice to share it with you." He leaned down and kissed me gently. I kissed him back, wanting more. His arms wrapped around me, and I got so lost in the kiss it took me a moment to realize we were flying. I pulled away. "Levi!"

He laughed. "Unlike you, I can do two things at the same time."

We got back to the house in no time.

"Do you want to shower first, or should I?" Levi asked as soon as we took off our muddy shoes and had some water.

"What, no third option for taking them at the same time?" It wasn't like Levi to pass up the opportunity for sexual innuendo.

"I didn't want to push my luck."

"Too bad. I would have chosen that option." I put down my glass and headed down the hall to our room.

He coughed. Some water probably went down the wrong tube. "That option is definitely on the table."

"No thanks. I don't want you to think that I'm pressuring you."

"You're going to kill me, girl. Kill me."

"I know," I called behind me as I closed myself in the bathroom. I had to take a minute to slow my breathing. I let the water run, filling the room with steam before pulling out my toiletries and getting in.

I shaved, and enjoyed a few more minutes in the warm water before getting out.

Levi was waiting in the bedroom.

"Your turn."

"Thanks." He kissed me on the cheek, and then my neck. "If you change your mind, and want to join me, I won't hold it against you."

"Have a good shower."

He turned the water on, and I started getting ready. I'd gone for a simple, black strapless dress, figuring you could never go wrong with a little, black dress.

I zipped it up most of the way, but couldn't get it all of the way up.

Levi had turned off the water, so I knocked on the door once. "Can I come in?"

"Be my guest."

I pushed open the door and almost closed it again. He was standing by the sink, a towel tied around his waist. He looked way too good with his hair wet.

He was definitely amused by my appraisal. "Need some help with that zipper?"

I looked over at him again, a few drops of water trailed down his chest, and I was undone.

"No, I don't think I need help with it after all." I let go, letting my dress fall down to my feet.

I looked down at the dress before stepping out of it and making myself meet his eyes.

"The dress looked pretty, but I like you better this way."

"Really? I thought you'd like this better." I took a deep breath, knowing that there would be no turning back from what I was about to do. I reached around and unclasped my strapless bra.

His eyes widened. "You're right, I like that even better."

He closed the space between us, his lips claiming mine with a fierceness I wasn't expecting.

He carried me over to the bed, and somewhere between the bathroom, and laying me down, he'd lost the towel. "I like this side of you, Al."

"The naked side, or the take-charge side?"

"Both. Definitely both." He pulled off my panties, before laying down next to me. "I really hope this isn't another dream."

"Am I usually like this in your dreams?"

"You're usually naked…"

"What a coincidence, you're usually naked in mine, too."

He smiled. "I knew you dreamed about me."

"Enough dream talk." I pulled his face to mine. "Kiss

me."

"Yes, Ma'am."

He kissed me again, letting his hands wander, reminding me of just how much I'd been missing.

Chapter Eighteen

"Maybe we should skip the dinner." Levi pulled me tighter against him.

"We can't, can we?" I asked, never wanting to leave the bed. The last time we'd gotten out of bed after having sex had been the beginning of the end. I didn't want another end.

"Technically we can, but we shouldn't…"

"Yeah, it wouldn't exactly leave a good impression."

"But, we can pick right back up where we are after dinner."

"And where are we exactly?"

"Where we're supposed to be."

"There are no more surprises, right?" Part of me still couldn't accept that I'd just slept with Levi again. If there was any doubt that we were really together, I erased it when I took my clothes off for him.

"Not like you're thinking. I already told you, no mind control, okay?"

"Okay."

I reluctantly picked my head up off his chest and went in search of my clothes. Thankfully, my dress wasn't too wrinkled from lying in a heap on the floor.

"I can't believe I gave in so quickly."

"Quickly? You call this quickly?" He pulled on his pants.

"I mean, so early in the weekend."

"I told you it was going to happen eventually, didn't I?" Was cocky Levi back already?

"Say 'I told you so' and you're not getting dessert."

"If you're talking about the dessert I think you are, my lips are sealed."

"Good."

He put a hand on my waist. "But don't pretend you don't want dessert. That game isn't going to work anymore."

"Okay, no 'I told you so' and no talk of games."

"You're so hot when you get flustered."

"I'm not flustered." I crossed my arms.

"Sure you're not."

"Whatever. I need to finish getting ready." I suppressed a smile. His cockiness could be annoying—but underneath it, I knew he was thrilled, and I was glad to be the cause of that.

My hair had mostly dried, so I didn't bother to tame it. I twisted it up into a bun, and I put on some simple makeup.

Levi had already left the room when I finished. I found a small box sitting on the dresser where I'd left my watch and earrings before getting in the shower. I opened the box and found a pair of dangle earrings made up of diamonds and red rubies. They were gorgeous. I touched one for a moment before putting it on. The last time I'd accepted jewelry from him my life had changed.

I slipped into my black kitten heels and found Levi in the kitchen.

"Well, hello there, gorgeous."

"These earrings are just earrings, right?"

"Yes, you like them?"

"Love them."

"Well, I love you." It was the third time he'd said the words, and although he said them casually, I could tell by the intensity of his gaze that he desperately wanted me to say them back to him.

I'd said the words to a boy before. I'd said them to Toby so many times that they became nothing more than a greeting. Still, admitting my feelings to Levi was a big step, and I knew it was time to take it. "I love you, too."

His eyes lit up. "I'm glad you've finally realized it."

"You really act like an arrogant prick sometimes, you know that?"

"Yes, but you love me anyway."

"True." I turned to rifle through the cabinets for a snack. I'd planned to eat after my shower, but hadn't exactly gotten that far.

I settled on a granola bar. "You want one?"

"Sure."

I tossed him one with chocolate chips.

"Is it bad that we're snacking before this thing?"

"No, you need to eat tonight. You'll need your energy later."

"On that note, let's go." I threw my wrapper in the garbage, picked up my purse, and headed to the door.

***

For the first time, I actually felt like a princess. Everyone rose to their feet as I walked in on Levi's arm.

"We are so honored to have you," a woman said before curtseying to me.

I wasn't quite sure how to respond, but I figured a simple thank you could go a long way. "Thank you so much for having me."

"We'd heard you were lovely, but the prince has certainly made a good choice." A man smiled before taking my hand and kissing it.

Levi stiffened, and the man dropped my hand. "I'm sorry, Sir. Forgive me."

Levi merely nodded at him and pulled me along further into the room. At first glance, it looked like a room full of regular people, but I knew most of them were anything but human.

It might have been Levi's first time presiding, but he clearly knew what he was doing. I figured he must have gone with his dad before. He stopped at a small table with only two seats, and pulled one out for me. I sat down and let him push me in.

He stood in front of his chair and addressed the room. "You may be seated."

As everyone else sat, he took his seat next to me. If it was a wedding, we'd have been at our sweethearts table.

"No cocktail hour first?" I whispered.

"That's after dinner."

"Oh…"

"So, I probably should have warned you, but we're going to be sharing tonight," he said so quietly, I could barely hear him.

"Sharing?" I whispered.

"Do you see a plate in front of you?"

I looked down and sure enough there wasn't one. "We're using one plate?"

"It's an old tradition symbolizing the complete connection between a royal and his mate."

"Well, you better not give me cooties," I pouted.

"It's a little late for that."

"Still… Okay, so I get the one plate thing, but I only see one set of silverware."

"That's because I'm going to be feeding you."

My jaw dropped. "Please tell me you're joking."

"Afraid not."

"For future notice, you will not drop these weird traditions on me last minute."

He leaned across the table slightly. "Telling you

wouldn't change anything."

"I'd have been prepared."

"Sir, may I serve you some wine?" I glanced up to see a waiter at Levi's elbow.

Levi examined the unopened bottle. "Yes."

Levi tasted it before nodding at the waiter to let him know he approved.

As soon as the waiter walked away, Levi proposed a toast. "To us."

"To us," I echoed before taking a sip. At least we each got our own glass.

After one spoonful of the seafood bisque, I was tired of being fed. Levi was enjoying it way too much, especially since everyone was watching us.

"I'm going to save room."

I didn't enjoy being served the main course of glazed duck with a rice pilaf and grilled vegetables, but I admit that I let Levi feed me more than my share of the dark chocolate and raspberry torte for dessert.

"So now we stay for a cocktail hour?"

"Pretty much. It's going to be like a meet and greet." He used his napkin to dab a little bit of chocolate off my lip.

"I have my own napkin."

"It's my fault you have it on your lips. I might as well clean you up." He smirked.

"You do realize I'm not going to let you feed me every time."

"We'll see."

He took my hand and led me to another room. A large bar at the back of the space was the only furniture, otherwise it was just open.

"Levi, it's wonderful to see you again," an attractive brunette crooned. "And your mate is absolutely lovely."

"Thank you, Gloria," Levi said politely, but he pulled me closer to his side.

"I'm sure you've already been over your roster for

tomorrow, but I have a case before you. I hope you take our families long history into consideration."

"I'm sorry, but you know I can't let personal connections influence my decisions."

"Of course not, you're a good man, just like your father."

"Exactly." He tensed at the mention of his father. He was more nervous than I thought.

"Nice meeting you," I said, pulling Levi with me.

"What was that about?" I whispered.

"She's a witch who had a fling with my uncle years ago."

"A witch?"

"Yes, a witch. Although some choose to stay outside The Society, they have to register with us if they want to use any magic."

"So formal."

"Very."

"Excuse me, I hate to interrupt, but I wanted to take the opportunity to introduce myself." A stout man with a completely pale face and a top hat held out his hand to Levi. He took off his hat before bowing awkwardly.

"Hello, may I get your name?"

"Oh yes, Harold Mayer. I am the new representative of the Bleths."

"Well, nice to meet you, Harold."

Levi led me away without introducing us. "What's a Bleth?"

"A Shifter-Dryad hybrid."

"Dryad? Like a Nymph?"

"Yes."

"But aren't they supposed to be really pretty?"

"Yes. Pure Dryads are, but the Nymph genes can only do so much with the genes of an ugly animal." He tried to keep a straight face.

"What kind of animal is he a shifter of?"

"A porcupine."

"You've got to be kidding."

He shook his head. "Nope, there are even rat shifters you know…"

I cringed. "Lovely. I'm glad you're not one."

"So am I, love. So am I."

By the time Levi met and shook hands with everyone at the party, I thought I was going to fall over. Had I known how much standing we'd be doing, I'd have worn flats.

I was contemplating going in search of a chair when everyone in the room bowed slightly.

"Our cue." Levi took my arm and led me from the room and out to the car.

"Can we go home now?"

"Anxious are you?" He arched an eyebrow.

"Not for the reason you think."

He opened my door, and hesitated before closing it. "No? Are you sure about that?"

"Positive. I just needed to get off my feet," I challenged. There was no way I was giving up that easily.

"We'll see about that." He closed my door and went around to the driver's side.

The drive took longer than I expected. "Are you lost?"

"No."

"Are you sure?"

"Absolutely. I just wanted to go for a drive." He grinned.

"Levi, this isn't funny." We were on some dark back road, and all I wanted to do was get changed and into bed—preferably with Levi next to me.

"Tell me the truth, and I'll be done driving."

"The truth? Are we really playing this game?"

"Apparently. I really thought we were finally done with the games though."

"I wasn't lying. I needed to get off my feet."

"But is that the only reason you were in a hurry to get home?"

"No," I admitted.

"I'm listening."

"Why should I have to say anything? You're not."

"You want me to tell you why I want to get home? Not a problem. I want to get home so I can undress you and get you into bed underneath me." He placed a hand on my leg, slowly moving it under the fabric of my dress. "Your turn."

I closed my eyes, loving how nice his hand felt, and thinking about the hours we'd spent together in bed earlier. "I want you. Is that what you want to hear?"

"Exactly what I wanted to hear. Open communication is important to a healthy relationship."

I shook my head. "Take me home."

"My pleasure."

Levi made another turn and within five minutes we were pulling up out front of the guest house. He hadn't moved his hand the whole time, and I felt its absence when he removed it to get out. He must have noticed my expression. "Don't worry. I'll have my hands all over you in about a minute."

He came around to open my door. "Make that thirty seconds." He picked me up and carried me inside, slamming the door and locking it behind us.

He carried me right to the bedroom. "Now where were we?"

"Right here." I smiled, as he laid me down on the bed.

CHAPTER NINETEEN

Levi looked fantastic in his suit. He always looked nice dressed up, but his excitement made him look even better. I'd settled on a pair of black dress pants and a pink merino wool sweater. I'd correctly assumed the court chambers would be freezing—paranormals seemed to always run a few degrees warmer than humans.

I was seated in a cushioned chair that might be described as a throne. My chair was only separated from Levi's by a few inches, and it was weird to be sitting in such a position of authority.

A tall man who had introduced himself as Ray had a long list written on parchment that, when unfolded, went all the way to the floor. If it weren't for the fact that the guy was young, and in shape, it would have been like looking at Santa with his naughty and nice list. I snickered, picturing Ray with a hat and coat.

Levi looked at me. "What's so funny?"

"Nothing."

"Tell me."

It was hard to keep anything from Levi after the night we'd shared. "I was picturing Ray as Santa."

He grinned. "A Pteron Santa…interesting."

"So he is a Pteron… I wondered."

"Yup, he's our point man here."

"Levi, are you ready?" Ray interrupted nervously.

"Of course." Levi kissed my cheek before straightening in his chair to face the front of the room.

"First up is Norman Taylor, a Were."

"Very well," Levi said formally.

An older man with sandy hair approached the elevated platform where we sat. He bowed slightly. "Thank you for the opportunity to present my grievances."

"It is your right."

"As you know, the Canton pack has claim to the land directly east of Baton Rouge."

Levi nodded. "Yes, I understand you have rights to the land."

"We've repeatedly caught members of the Talbot Coven on our land. Ordinarily, we wouldn't find a need to address the royal court, but we believe they are using spells against some of our men."

"What evidence do you have?"

"The words of the men themselves. They've been waking up in the woods with only blurred memories of what happened."

"Is that the only evidence?"

"No." Norman turned red.

"What is it?"

"I don't know if I should say it in front of your mate, Sir."

"You know it is proper to have her present."

"Of course. I will continue."

Levi nodded.

"The men have only vague memories of engaging in activities with the women of the coven."

"Activities?" Levi smiled slightly. "Are you trying to say that the men have had sex with coven members?"

"Yes." Norman looked down at the ground.

"Is there a member of the Talbot Coven present?"

"Yes, Sir." Gloria, the brunette from the night before, strode forward.

I watched, completely transfixed. This was better than any soap opera.

"Hello, Gloria. What do you have to say to his claim?"

"It's true."

"You are admitting that members of your coven trespassed on Were land and used spells against them?"

"No. I'm admitting that members of my coven have had sexual relations with members of his pack. The last time I checked, sex between paranormals wasn't a violation of any rule."

Norman interrupted. "It is when it's coerced."

"Coerced? Do most men have to be coerced into sex?" she purred.

"Sir, I beg you to put her in line. I run my pack traditionally. My men must find mates within the pack, or join with women from other Were groups. They do not fraternize with witches."

A faint smile played on the corners of Levi's lips. "I don't really have anything to say to that, so I'm going to stick to the hard and fast rules. Gloria, do you admit your members were on pack land without permission?"

"Define permission." She smiled.

"Answer the question."

"Yes. But, I'm not aware of any coven members using magic there. They were only after a drink and a good time."

"A drink?"

"Yes. Norman's generation might run things traditionally, but their sons don't. There have been some pretty wild parties lately."

"Okay. I think I've heard enough. Gloria, keep your members off Were land, okay?"

"Not a problem. But while I'm addressing you, my coven has our own grievance."

"Is it on the list?" Levi asked Ray.

"Yes, she's on the list."

"Norman, are you satisfied?"

"Yes, Sir." He looked away, clearly embarrassed.

I was using all my power to keep myself from laughing. I couldn't imagine a Were and witch orgy. Who knew what was really happening in this world I had only recently been introduced to.

"Okay, Gloria, what's your issue?"

"We seek a license for unrestricted spell commerce."

A hush fell through the crowd watching the proceedings.

Levi shifted in his seat. "On what grounds do you make that request?"

"We need it. The current regulations are too stringent."

"Is that all you have to say?"

"Face it, Levi. The economy has ruined all of us. If we don't expand our markets, we're going under."

"I'd prefer if you didn't address me so informally," he said tersely.

"Fine, Sir."

"I will take your request into consideration and send a response within fourteen days, as usual."

"Thank you, Sir." She bowed slightly and walked away.

At first I couldn't take my eyes off the proceedings, but as the hours wore on, I had trouble keeping my eyes open. Hearing about land disputes between paranormal groups got tiring after a while. I must have dozed off.

"Ready, sleepyhead?"

"Hmm?" I blinked, trying to remember where I was. I looked around and realized we were still in the court room.

"Wow, that's embarrassing."

Levi laughed. "I would have done it myself if I could have. I don't know about you, but I'm starving. How about we head home? I did promise to make you dinner, didn't I?"

"Oh yeah." I got up, stretched for a second, and

followed Levi out of the now empty chamber.

Back in the car, he turned to me. "So what did you think?"

"I thought it was pretty cool at first. You were definitely very royal." I laughed. "But, obviously, the novelty wore off."

"Yeah, I bet. Thanks for sitting with me though."

"It's not like it helped."

"Are you kidding?"

"No…"

"First, I never would have been allowed to preside if we weren't mated. Second, the fact that you came gave me so much more authority."

I turned in my seat. "Why?"

"A royal is only as strong as his bloodline. Having a beautiful, young mate reassures my subjects that the line is going to continue."

"They better not expect an heir anytime soon."

He laughed, but it sounded forced. "Some probably do. We have some traditionalists that would have a fit if they knew you were using birth control."

I bristled. "Why would that be any of their business?"

"It isn't, obviously, but that doesn't stop them from thinking it is."

I looked out the window.

"Let's change the subject. It's nothing worth worrying about now. We have years."

"Good idea. So what are you making me for dinner?"

"Pizza."

"Please tell me it's not the frozen kind."

We were just pulling into the gravel driveway. "Of course not. Give me some credit, babe."

It definitely wasn't a frozen pizza. With a glass of wine in hand, I watched as Levi tossed the dough and made a spinach and chicken pizza. I was impressed he remembered it was my favorite kind. We sat at the counter while we waited for it to cook, and it felt so nice to just do something laid back together.

While Levi pulled out the pizza, I finished off the salad. We had a quiet dinner and ended up sitting by the fire pit outside. Levi brought out some blankets and we curled up together on a deep couch with plush cushions looking up at the star-filled sky.

"Thanks for dinner."

"I'm glad you liked it." He played with a strand of my hair.

"I'm glad I came."

"So am I." He leaned over and kissed me gently on the lips. "So glad."

His arms came around me as the light kiss became so much more. I moved onto his lap, straddling him. His hand slipped under my sweater and bra, cupping a breast. I sighed and leaned into him. I put a hand up the back of his t-shirt, running my fingers over the slightly raised bumps that lined the slits that were the only evidence of his wings.

I broke the kiss. "Do you remember what I asked you the last time I was in your lap like this?"

His lips turned into a smile. "Yes, I do."

"Want to?"

He nodded, using his free hand to pull off his t-shirt.

"Wait, out here?"

"Why not? There's no one around for miles."

"It's cold."

"You're not going to be cold for long."

"I won't?"

"I assure you, I'll be keeping you warm." He let the blanket fall off my shoulders, and moved his other hand to pull my sweater over my head. He unclasped my bra, and wasted no time before letting his hands and mouth cover the newly exposed skin. I was so distracted that I barely noticed him removing the rest of our clothes before laying me down. He hovered above me, just close enough that I could wrap my arms around his neck.

My hands were twisted in his hair when he took one

and moved it onto his back. I felt the firm feathers, and looked in awe at the beautiful black wings. "Amazing."

He smiled, and kissed me before positioning himself over me.

I knew instantly something was different. Sex was always incredible with him, but what I was experiencing put each of the other times to shame. I dug my hands into his back, needing him even closer.

"I love you, Al. I love you so much." His lips attacked my neck, and I bit my lip to stop from screaming out.

"Don't hold back, no one's here."

I looked into his eyes, shocked to see they were black. I couldn't focus on them long and finally gave up keeping quiet.

***

We'd been lying under a blanket for at least five minutes before I finally spoke. "That was better than flying."

"I agree with you there."

Levi's wings were still extended, and I reached out to touch one. "That was incredible."

"You were incredible."

"Did you know you transformed?" I asked tentatively. I really wasn't sure what that meant, if anything.

"I know...I felt it. I didn't hurt you, did I?" He used a hand to move my chin up to look at him.

"No, not at all."

"Good. I knew it would probably be better, but not like that."

"How'd you know?"

"My dad."

"Your dad? You talked to your dad about this?"

He laughed. "Not exactly. It's more like he talked to me about it. It was part of his speech about how great it was to find a mate. That way you could actually be yourself."

"Well, we're definitely doing that again."

"Are we?"

His hand moved down toward my chest but I stopped it. "Not now."

"No?"

"Nope. Right now, all I want to do is cuddle. I'm still recovering."

"I can cuddle. You've given me a lot of experience with that."

"Cuddling after sex is more fun though, right?"

"Much more fun. I prefer getting those annoying clothes out of the way." He pulled me closely against him, and I closed my eyes, just enjoying how good it felt to be naked in his arms.

CHAPTER TWENTY

"Good morning, love."

"Morning." We were back in our bed inside. Levi must have moved us while I slept.

"What time is it?"

"Nine. I must have tired you out last night. You slept like a rock...mostly."

"Mostly?"

"You did say my name one or two times."

"Seriously? I need to stop doing that." Surprisingly, it didn't embarrass me.

"No. Definitely not. Keep those dreams coming. It means I'm doing something right."

"You definitely did something right last night."

"Did I?"

"Yes... it's probably good I fell asleep so quickly, otherwise I would have kept you up."

He laughed. "I wouldn't have minded."

"Did you sleep well?" I asked belatedly.

"Very well."

"But you must have been up awhile if you heard me talking."

"I slept more than usual. I usually only get three or four hours. I probably got seven last night."

"Three or four hours? How do you function?"

"I technically only need to sleep a few hours a week…"

"What?" I sat up. "What else don't I know about you?"

"Do my sleep habits really upset you that much?" He pulled me back down into bed next to him.

"No, it's just that I wish I knew more about you."

"Like what?"

"Do you need to eat?"

"Yes, I need to eat."

I snuggled into the sheets. "But how much. Is it like sleep?"

"No, I need to eat as much as you. Scratch that—more than you."

"What about—"

"Don't ask about the bathroom, that's the same too."

"Levi."

"What?"

"Okay, I know you can see well in the dark, but you don't have x-ray vision or anything, do you?"

"Are you asking whether I can see through your clothes?"

"Maybe."

"No, unfortunately not."

"Good."

"Good? Would that really bother you? I already know exactly how good you look naked…" He pulled away the blanket to look at me.

I pushed the blanket back down. "It's not me I'm worried about."

"Wow, that would make you jealous, huh?" He grinned. "Don't worry, babe. Even if I could, no one would hold a candle to you." Something about the way he said it, and the intense way he looked at me, made me believe him.

"We have to go back to school, don't we?"

"We still have another few days of study break. We can stay another night."

I sat up on an elbow. "But I need to study."

"You can study here. Didn't you drag all your books?"

"Maybe."

His phone rang, interrupting our conversation.

"Hi Dad. Yes, it's been fine."

I figured it was going to be a long conversation, so I decided to take a shower. My heart nearly jumped out of my chest when Levi joined me a few minutes later. "You made me shower alone yesterday. You're not doing it again."

"Well, then, make yourself useful." I handed him the soap. Levi brought out such a strong and sexy side of me I never realized I had.

"Yes, Ma'am." He grinned, and I was ready to agree to another night in Shreveport.

Those plans were dashed when he filled me in on his talk with his dad. He'd just finished drying me off. He insisted on doing it himself. "So, it looks like you'll get back to study after all."

I tried to hide my disappointment. "Oh, does your dad need you back?"

"Actually, he wants to see both of us."

"Really?"

"Yeah, he wants us at dinner at their place tonight."

I hadn't been to his parents' house since the party in August, and then it was only the backyard.

"Don't look so nervous. It's not a big deal."

"It's a big enough deal that he wants us back right away." I rifled through my suitcase for some clothes.

"I think he just wants to talk about how things went. He sounded happy with me though. This is a good thing."

I forced a smile. "All right, do I get breakfast or are we leaving immediately?" I pulled on a sweater.

"Breakfast sounds good. What do you want?"

"Do you think you have pancake mix? I'm craving

some."

"I bet we do. Let's look." I followed him out to the kitchen. After rifling through the cabinets, he pulled out the mix, along with the milk and eggs from the fridge.

I opened the freezer, glad to find some frozen blueberries.

"You like blueberry pancakes, too?" He turned from the stove.

"Love them."

After stuffing ourselves with blueberry pancakes, we packed up and got back in the car. The ride home was pleasant enough, but it went too quickly. I wasn't ready to face my friends at school, or worse, Levi's parents.

He pulled up by my dorm. "Thanks for an amazing time, Al."

"Thank you."

He leaned over to kiss me. "I'll be back to get you at seven."

"You'll bring my car back to the hotel?"

"After I clean it."

"You better." I moved to open my door.

"Al?"

I turned back to look at him.

"Pack whatever you need for tonight and tomorrow. I want you staying at my place."

I hesitated for a moment. I wanted to spend another night with him, but I also wanted to make sure I got to catch up with my friends. I couldn't decide. "Maybe." I got out.

I took two steps away from the car before he caught up with me. I hadn't expected him to get out. He backed me up so I was leaning against the car. "No maybe. Yes. You can't just cut me off."

I laughed. "You can handle it. I'll think about it."

"Pack a bag, Al, or don't complain to me when you have to use my toothbrush."

I made a face. "I'll see you later."

"Aren't you forgetting something?"

"What?"

He opened the tailgate and pulled out my bag.

"Oh yeah," I reached for the suitcase.

He pulled it away. "Like I'm going to make you carry it."

I shrugged. "Suit yourself."

I used my ID to swipe into the dorm and Levi followed me up the steps. I unlocked my door, not surprised to find Hailey studying on her bed. She rarely used her desk anymore.

"Hey!" She got up and hugged me. "How was the trip?"

"Good." I smiled.

"Only good?" Levi moved into the room.

I glared at him.

"I guess I can just ask you, Levi. How was the weekend?"

"Fantastic. Allie and I got to spend a lot of quality time together."

"I bet." Hailey gave me a knowing look.

"See you at seven." Levi gave me a kiss before walking out.

"Bye." I waved.

"What's at seven?"

"Dinner with the Laurents." I pulled off my sweatshirt, hanging it up in my closet.

"Ohh, fancy."

"Shut up."

"So tell me, what happened?"

I sat down on my bed facing her. "A lot."

"Can you be more specific than that?"

I picked up a heart shaped pillow that Anne had left at some point. "We're officially back together."

"No wonder he looked like a kid in a candy store."

"Yeah, well, it was bound to happen, right?"

She closed her book, no longer even pretending she

was going back to it. "So was it as good as you remembered?"

"Better."

"Good thing Levi left, or you'd be giving him even more of an ego."

"Oh, don't worry, that's already happened."

"You're back!" Our door flung open and Anne ran in, followed by Tiffany, who gave me an apologetic look.

"Yeah, I've been back a whole ten minutes now."

Anne bent down and hugged me. "It's been too quiet without you."

I laughed. "It's nice to know I was missed."

"Oh my god, you finally did it." Anne grinned as she sat down next to me on my bed.

"What? Am I wearing an 'I had sex' sign or something?"

"It's the glow. The 'I spent the last few days shacked up with the sexy guy I've been holding back on' glow."

Hailey snickered. "I don't think they spent the whole time in bed."

"It was a business trip, right?" Tiffany asked, sitting on Hailey's chair.

"Yes, an important business trip Levi needed her company on." Anne rolled her eyes.

"Fine, don't believe me."

"Oh, I do, but I don't think Levi cared about the business."

"He did. It was the most responsibility his dad has ever given him."

"You know you can tell us about it if you want, Allie. We already know who he is." Tiffany smiled.

Sometimes I forgot they were in on the secret, but I still didn't know how much to tell them. I looked to Hailey to get her take. She nodded.

"He had to preside over a paranormal court."

Anne took a sip from the pink cup she always seemed to carry around with her. "That sounds so formal."

"It was. It was fun at first, but I actually fell asleep."

"Seriously? You fell asleep?" Hailey asked.

"Yeah, Levi didn't seem to care though."

Hailey stretched out on her bed. "I would have paid to see that."

"Thanks, I appreciate it."

"Come on, you fell asleep at court, that's pretty bad."

I leaned back on my elbows. "It was seven hours, and all I could do was sit there."

"Or sleep," Hailey teased.

"Could you stop making fun of me long enough to help me pick out something to wear?"

"To wear to what?" Anne asked.

"Allie's got dinner with Levi's parents tonight."

"Dinner with any guy's parents is rough, but I'm guessing royalty would be worse. Good luck." Anne smiled sympathetically.

"Sometimes I worry you have multiple personalities," I teased.

"What?"

"One minute you're egging me on, and the next you're being all understanding."

"Hey, it's called being your friend."

"I know."

Tiffany interrupted. "So let's get back to the real issue. What are you wearing?"

"That's the problem. I don't know. I feel like Helen always looks so dressy, so I need to dress up, right?"

"I'd go with a simple skirt and sweater. It could go either way." Tiffany was already heading over to my closet.

I nodded. "That's what I was thinking."

Hailey joined Tiffany and was flipping through my clothes. "Hmm, maybe a dress? I haven't been to dinner at their house, but I'm guessing it's pretty formal."

"Why not just call and ask Levi?" Anne fidgeted with her watch. "It's his parents."

"That would be the easy solution, but he'd probably

just tell me to wear something short and red."

Hailey laughed. "So, then, just wear what you want."

"I will. But I need to study first. Anyone want to grab coffee and head over to the library?"

"I'm up for the coffee part..." Tiffany said. "I'm sick of studying though."

"All right, that works."

Anne looked like she was considering the question carefully. "I'm up for both."

"Hail?"

"Have you ever seen me turn down caffeine?"

"Good point."

We grabbed sweatshirts and headed over to the Rue, one of the campus coffee shops.

I sipped my mocha while catching up with my friends. Mostly everyone was excited about vacation. Anne and Tiffany were excited about going home, but I still didn't know what I was going to do. I'd been avoiding my mom's calls, knowing she'd want to know what day to expect me. Her messages said something about skiing in Vermont. There was no way she was going to take no for an answer again, but I didn't feel like I was ready to bring Levi home. Unfortunately, I knew with certainty I wasn't going to be allowed to go alone.

"Hey Allie, wait a sec," Hailey said as we got ready to head to the library. She gestured for the others to go ahead.

"Yeah?"

"If you want me to go home with you over break, you just have to ask."

"I couldn't ask. It's Christmas. You're supposed to be with your family."

She took a sip of her coffee. "You spent Thanksgiving with mine. I can spend Christmas with yours."

"Won't your family mind, or think it's weird you're going instead of Levi?"

"No, they'll get it."

"Well, thanks. I'll think about it."

"Good."

***

Two hours later, we packed up our books and headed back to the dorm. I decided on a V-neck black dress, figuring I'd rather be overdressed than under.

"You look great." Levi grinned when he saw me. He was wearing a sports coat, making me instantly glad I'd gone for the dress.

He opened the car door for me. "So this is okay for tonight then?"

"Your dress? It's perfect."

I tried to push away the nerves as we drove over. If Levi noticed, he didn't say anything. All too soon, he pulled up in front of his large, white house. With tall columns and wrap around porches, it was the kind of house you expected to see in a magazine. He took my hand, and I found myself walking into a two-story foyer. Without a word, he moved behind me and took off my cardigan. I shivered a little, my bare skin not used to the temperature of the house.

"Hi, honey." Helen greeted Levi with a hug, before pulling me into one too.

"Hi, Helen." I smiled and saw Robert coming from over her shoulder.

Robert stopped right next to us. "Allison, looking lovely as always."

"Thank you." I fought myself to make eye contact. He still made me so nervous.

"Come in, come in. We haven't talked much lately." Helen led me into a formal living room. Out of the corner of my eye, I noticed Levi and his dad disappearing into another room.

Helen must have noticed me looking. "Robert and Levi need to chat about your trip."

"Oh, okay," I said absently. Really I was trying to take in all of the details of the place.

"Can I get you something to drink?" Helen stopped in front of a small bar.

"Only if you're fixing something for yourself."

"How about a glass of wine? We'll need to open some for dinner anyway."

"Perfect."

She opened a bottle and poured two glasses. I settled into a cream loveseat while I waited. Helen came to sit down in a chair across from me.

"So, tell me, how was the trip?"

"It was interesting."

"I know those proceedings can be really boring, but it's important that Levi had you there."

"I don't really get why. I don't see how having me there makes him look more powerful."

Helen smiled and took a sip of her red wine. "Don't ever forget your importance. Levi needs you."

"I wonder if he knows that."

"He does. Trust me."

"What do I know?" Levi put his hands on my shoulders. The contact warmed me.

"How important Allie is to you."

He bent down and whispered in my ear. "Oh, I know."

"Are you two ready?" Helen asked.

"Yeah, Dad's already in the dining room." Levi came around to take my hand and walked me to the other room. I glanced back and saw his mom beaming as she looked at us.

I was half expecting a servant to bring in the food, but Helen placed four bowls of salad on the table. "I hope you like steak, sweetie. These two always want meat."

"Yes, I eat everything," I answered quickly.

Robert turned his attention to me. "Allie, I'm glad you were able to join us tonight. I have been meaning to talk to you about something."

I tensed. I doubted anything he had to say was good.

"How set are you on continuing your studies at Tulane after this year?"

"Do you mean whether I want to transfer?" Where was this coming from?

"Not exactly. It's just that there are a lot of great online programs available now."

"Online programs? What is this about?" I looked at Levi but his face was blank.

"Levi and I were just discussing your plans after he graduates and you get married this summer."

Married...I knew Robert thought that, but it was strange to actually hear him say it.

"Levi's going to be taking over international relations for me starting in August."

"International relations?"

"Yes. You two will have the opportunity to see a lot of the world."

"And how does my education fit in? You don't expect me to drop out of school, do you?"

"I already mentioned online opportunities." Robert looked at me with just a hint of a smile.

"I want to be a biochemistry major. I can't take all of those classes online."

"I'm sure you'll find something more suitable to that environment then." His smile became more of a sneer, and for the first time, I was able to see beneath his charm to something else entirely.

"Helen, let's eat please." Robert's demand let me know our talk was over.

Levi gave me a quick glance, as if to warn me to stay quiet.

I barely touched my dinner, only pushing the meat around on the plate to avoid offending Helen. As I sat there staring at my plate, I made a decision. If Levi didn't support me on this, then we were over.

"Would you like some dessert? Coffee?" Helen asked,

pulling me out of my thoughts.

"No, thank you. I really need to get back and study."

"Right now?" Levi finished off the last of his meal, placing his silverware down on the plate.

"Yes. If you want to stay, I'll just call a cab." I hoped he heard the coldness in my voice.

"No, I can take you." He jumped up.

I put my napkin on the table and pushed in my chair. "Thanks for dinner." I addressed only Helen. I couldn't stand to look at Robert. I didn't bother to get my cardigan.

"Hey, slow down." Levi caught up with me just as I reached his car.

I turned to face him. "Please tell me you don't agree with him. You're going to tell him there's no way I'm quitting school, right?"

He put his hands in his pockets, a decidedly non-Levi mannerism. "Allie, it's just a year. This is really important. And my dad's right, there are all sorts of online programs now."

I tried to swallow down the huge lump that was stuck in my throat. "I can't just get my biochem degree online. Didn't you hear anything I said?"

"Come on, get in the car. I'd rather they not watch us fighting." He gestured to the house.

I didn't particularly want them watching either, so I got in. He closed my door and got in himself, starting the engine just as I'd buckled my seatbelt.

"I'm waiting."

"For what?" He took his eyes off the road to look at me.

"Did you hear anything I said? I can't do labs online."

"You just decided on that major a few months ago. You can just change your mind again." I'm not sure if it was the actual words, or the fact that he didn't look at me when he said it that made me angrier.

"Stop the car!"

"No way, we're going back to my place."

I twisted my hands in my lap. "Not a chance in hell."

"Calm down."

"Calm down? You know how important school is to me!"

"And you'll get a degree one way or another. Who cares how you get it?"

My anger nearly choked me. "Either stop this car now, or I jump out while it's moving."

"I'd like to see that."

I fumbled with the automatic lock on my door, pushing it open.

Levi slammed on the brakes and pulled over. "Jesus, Allie."

"I warned you." I got out, needing to get as far away from Levi as possible.

"Calm down." He came around to my side of the car.

"No, I'm not going to calm down. You promised me I wouldn't have to give up anything else to be with you. Now you're asking me to drop out of school."

"No, I'm asking you to take classes in a different way."

"You got to do four years of college traditionally, why can't I? Why do I have to go with you?"

"And you say I don't listen?" He wrung his hands. "I can't do it without you. You are the symbol of my power. Get it through your head."

"The symbol of your power? What about my power?"

"Your power? A few months ago you didn't even know about The Society."

"I'm not talking about The Society. I'm talking about power over my own life. I finally move out from under my parents and now you do this to me?"

Levi finally looked at me. "Are you crying, Al?"

I nodded, and seconds later his arms came around me. "This is really important to you, isn't it?"

I tried to compose myself. "Yes."

"Then we'll figure something out."

I looked up at him from underneath wet eyelashes.

"You'll talk to your dad?"

"I think we can work this out ourselves." He brushed a few tears off my face.

"How?"

"I'm thinking. Maybe we can just pack your schedule with Tuesday/Thursday classes so you can take long weekends."

"And we're just going to travel the world on the weekends?"

He put a hand under my chin to make me look up at him. "I don't mind spending my Thursday nights on a private jet alone with you? Do you have any problem with it?"

"A private jet?"

"How did you think we were traveling? You thought I was going to fly you across the globe?"

"No, but…"

"Will you get back in the car now?"

I barely had the energy to stand. "Yes."

"Will you come home with me?"

"Not tonight. I really just need to catch my breath." Everything was happening too fast. I just wanted things to move at a normal pace.

"Tomorrow night then?"

"I have a final in two days."

"Normally I'd make a comment about how obsessive you are about school, but I'm guessing that would be a bad idea right now."

"You're learning."

"Come on. Let me get you to your dorm." With an arm around my shoulder, he led me back to the car. He bent down and gently kissed me before closing the door.

We rode back to campus in silence, but he had his hand on my leg the whole time. I think that was his way of letting me know we were okay.

He pulled to a stop in his usual spot. "I don't like fighting with you. Let's try to go a few days without it."

"I'd like that."

"Want to meet up and study tomorrow?"

"You want to study?" I didn't think Levi ever studied.

"Sure. We should probably go over art history."

"All right, what time?"

"Ten. We can go to breakfast first if you want."

"Then make it nine."

"Nine? Isn't that a little early?"

"Do you want to meet up or what?"

"Yes. I'll be there at nine."

"Perfect." I leaned over and kissed him.

"You sure you won't come home with me? It's not too late."

"Good night, Levi." I got out of the car smiling. We'd had a huge fight—but we'd gotten through it. Maybe things really could work between us.

CHAPTER TWENTY-ONE

"What do you mean you can't meet me?" I whispered loudly as I walked out of the stacks at the library. A few kids turned to glare at me as I walked past.

"I'm sorry. My dad needs me for something."

"Can you at least drop off my notebook?" I slumped down on a couch outside the glass doors. I was technically allowed to be on my phone now, but I still felt rude. A study group sat together a few feet away.

"Not now. I'll bring it by tonight though."

"But the Art History test is in the morning," I grumbled. I'd forgotten my notebook in his car after we'd studied the other day.

"I'm not in the city right now..."

"Oh, so how do you know you'll be back tonight?"

"Because I will."

"Fine. See you later."

"Men can be frustrating sometimes, can't they?" Michelle snuck up on me. She took a seat on the couch.

"Yeah, they can." I was too tired from studying to put on an act. It's not like a couple had to be happy one hundred percent of the time.

"I couldn't help but overhear your conversation. Levi has your art history notebook?"

"Yes. I left it at his place. And before you say it, I realize it wouldn't be an issue if I'd just take notes on a computer like everyone else."

She smiled. "I wasn't going to say that. But it's true..."

"Well, I probably should get back to trying to reread the entire text."

"Who's your professor? Is it Anders?"

"Yeah."

"I made a pretty awesome study guide when I had her last semester. I could send it to you."

"Really?" Then I thought about it for a second and my excitement waned. "Wait, why would you help me?"

She laughed dryly. "Okay, I know we didn't get off to the best start, but I'm not out to get you."

"And I should take your word because...?"

"What choice do you have?"

I shrugged. "None."

"For what it's worth, I'm sorry for being a bitch."

"What?"

"I was jealous, and I took it out on you. It wasn't cool. Okay?"

"You were jealous? Why?"

"I thought you had it easy. You got to spend your life with the guy you loved." She paused. "Funny, huh?"

I smiled. "Easy? That's a good one."

"But then I realized I had it wrong. I heard the rumors. I know what happened."

My chest tightened, here came the blackmail.

"Whoa, calm down."

I guess she read the panic on my face.

"Levi didn't tell you what you were getting yourself into, did he?"

I looked away, wishing I had a way out of the conversation.

"Everyone knows. *Everyone.*" She gave me a knowing

look.

"Everyone?"

She looked over her shoulder. Satisfied the study group wasn't listening she continued. "Even the king."

"Oh my god."

"He doesn't care. As long as you stay with Levi, it's fine. He's going to make sure you stay."

"It's not like I want to leave…Levi and I are making things work."

"But you don't really know how to handle it all, right?"

"I guess. I just need some time to think."

"Are you going home for break?"

"Kind of. I'm meeting my mom in Vermont. Hailey volunteered to come with me."

"She hates me, doesn't she?"

"She thinks you look down on her."

Michelle laughed. "Maybe I did, but I don't anymore."

"Good. If we're going to be friends, you're going to have to at least try to be friends with her too."

"I know. I'll go email you that study guide."

"Thanks."

"If I don't see you, enjoy the break."

"You too. Good luck on exams." I waved goodbye and shook my head in wonder. Michelle being nice?

***

"Pick up your phone or shut it off," Hailey grumbled.

I looked at my digital alarm clock. It was two thirty a.m.

I picked up my phone and squinted to read the display. Another missed call from Levi. Before I could put it back down, he sent a text.

I know it's late, but I have your notebook. Can you come down?

Late? It's the middle of the night.

Please come down.

Fine. I eventually relented. As annoyed as I was about

him ditching me, I couldn't deny how much I wanted to see him. I missed him, and I knew I'd probably miss him a whole lot more in the days to come. I needed time to clear my head, but that didn't mean I wasn't craving his presence.

He leaned against the wall outside, dressed in a tank and jeans. He must have flown. "Hey." He straightened out when he saw me.

"Hi." I pushed my glasses back toward my eyes.

"You're mad, aren't you?"

"You'd be dead, except Michelle saved you."

"Michelle?"

"Yeah, she gave me her study notes from last semester." I zipped up my hoodie, realizing how exposed I was since I hadn't bothered to put on a bra.

"So, in other words, I owe her."

"Yes."

"Well, here's this if you still want it." He held out my notebook.

"Want to know what to get me for Christmas?"

He smiled, probably thinking our previous discussion was over and he was off the hook. "Yes, although I'm probably going to surprise you anyway."

"An ultra-light laptop. Find me one to bring to class. This isn't happening again."

He laughed. "All right, I'll get you one. You've never asked me for anything before."

"You know how much I hate dealing with technology, and I won't be near an electronics store over break."

"Are you sure I can't come with you?" His expression suddenly turned serious.

"No. It's not because I don't want to spend the holidays with you, but I need time with my mom."

"If you change your mind, I can get there anytime."

"I know. We'll be back for New Years."

"Good. Otherwise I'd fly up there. We're definitely starting the New Year together."

"Sounds good." I yawned.

"All right, I'll let you go back to bed."

"How generous of you."

He leaned over and kissed me gently. "I'll see you at the final."

I smiled. "Don't forget, you have to take Hailey and me to the airport."

"I won't forget."

He kissed me again.

"If you don't cut that out, I'm not going to be able to go back to sleep."

"Ordinarily I'd say that's a good thing, but I don't want any more trouble."

"Good night, Levi."

"Good night."

Chapter Twenty-Two

My lips still felt swollen twenty minutes into our flight. Levi said he wanted to make sure I didn't forget him. I think he was hoping to make me stay, or at least beg him to come. It's not that I didn't want him to come, but I needed to take some time and slow things down. I also didn't want to deal with my mom's reaction yet.

"Could you quit making those lovey dovey faces? It's making me sick." Hailey playfully punched my arm.

"I am not making a lovey dovey face."

"If you say so."

I shifted in my seat trying to get comfortable. "I do. Can we talk about something other than Levi?" To be honest, thinking about Levi was a welcome distraction from thinking over my Art History exam. I completely blanked out on one of the pictures, and now I couldn't get it out of my head.

"You're acting like we've been talking about him for hours—just because you can't stop thinking about him doesn't mean I'm doing the same." She smiled.

"I appreciate you coming."

"It's not a problem. I'm excited to ski."

"I can't believe you've never been."

"I'm from New Orleans. How much skiing do you think we have?"

"Good point."

She took a sip from her bottle of water. "So are you going to ditch me on the bunny slopes, or are you going to join the humiliation with me."

"I'll be with you. But knowing you, you'll be on the double black diamonds by the end of the day."

"You're probably right."

"Does that come from being a Pteron?" I gestured to her. "Or is it just you."

"Probably both." She laughed.

***

I thought it would be my mom waiting for us at the tiny airport, but it was Andrew and the last person in the world I expected to see. "Oh my god."

"What?" Hailey followed my line of vision. "Is that our ride?"

"I can't do this." I stopped walking. People struggled to move by us.

"I assume one is the future step-brother, but who's the other?"

"Toby." I thought I might hyperventilate. I'm not one to panic, but this was bad. "And Andrew isn't my future step-brother." At least I hoped he wasn't.

"*The* Toby?"

"Yes." Somehow my ex-boyfriend was standing in the airport. I wasn't sure who was behind it, but I wasn't happy.

"Damn."

"My thoughts exactly."

"We'll get through this." Hailey touched my arm.

"I hope so." They hadn't seen us yet, and Toby paced anxiously.

"The only good thing is that at least Andrew's kind of cute." Hailey checked out the brown haired guy that liked to torture me in high school.

"Gag me." If she only knew how much of an annoying jerk he was growing up.

"He is. He kind of has the geeky hot thing going for him."

I was prevented from answering her when Andrew called my name. "Hey, Allie!"

At the sound of my name, Toby glanced over. He smiled and gave me a small wave.

"Hi, Andrew." I accepted his awkward hug, but really I couldn't take my eyes off Toby. I so didn't want to deal with him. This was supposed to be my time away to think about things with Levi. I didn't need Toby around.

"And hello to you." Andrew moved over to Hailey, picking up her left hand and kissing it. She giggled. Hailey never giggled.

I snickered and Toby took it as an invitation. "Hi, Allie." He stopped a few steps away from me.

"What are you doing here, Toby?"

"I needed to see you. You never came home for Thanksgiving, and Jess said you were coming up here."

"Jess? When did Jess tell you?" I'd only told her a few days earlier.

"She was with Emmett when you guys talked. He filled me in."

Of course, Emmett and Toby were practically best friends. "Oh." That's all I could muster.

"I've been a mess. When you didn't show up at school in August, I thought I'd die."

"Get real. We'd already been broken up for months." I looked over at the empty baggage conveyor belt, willing it to start.

"I didn't see it as a break up. I thought you just wanted some time."

"I never gave you any reason to think that." I crossed

my arms.

"Come on, Allie, you must have missed me. I know there's another guy, but he can't possibly be as good for you as I am."

I turned to look for Hailey. I'd gotten used to her saving me from awkward situations. She just shrugged. I guess there wasn't much she could do at the moment short of us getting back on a plane. "Even without Levi, we wouldn't be together."

"I don't believe that. Jess said that's why you stayed in New Orleans. If you'd have gone to Princeton, we'd be back together by now."

I shook my head. "No. We weren't meant to be."

"How can you say it like that? I love you. And you love me."

How could I respond to that? I thought I'd loved him, but now I wasn't sure I ever did. But how could I say that to the first boy who ever made my heart race, who I'd slept with more times than I could count. A boy who knew so many of my secrets, who knew what made me tick. "We're over, Toby."

"See, you can't even say it. You can't say you don't love me."

A loud beep announced that the baggage was about to start coming out. I used it as an excuse to get some space between us. I walked over to wait.

"I've been here since eight a.m."

I turned to look at him. "Why?"

"I only knew you were getting in today, not what time. I looked it up, and there was one flight originating in New Orleans, switching in Atlanta, that landed at nine thirty."

"Oh. I thought you just came with Andrew."

"You think I invited your ex-boyfriend to spend Christmas with us?" Andrew butted in. "That would be pretty low."

"So my mom doesn't know Toby's here?"

Andrew shook his head. "I didn't know until I found

him waiting."

"Good." At least I didn't have to be mad at the people I was spending the week with.

"You look great." Toby's voice came from right behind me. He pressed his body against my back, using the crowd as an excuse to get close. "But, then again, you always look great."

It was strange being so close to him again. It was familiar and comfortable in a way I didn't like. "I don't know what you were expecting, but I have a feeling you're going to be disappointed."

"I wasn't expecting anything. I just needed to see you."

I watched the sea of black bags moving around the belt. I noticed the pink tag I'd tied around the handle of my rolling suitcase and reached for it. Toby placed a hand over mine. "I've got it."

I backed up and let him pull it off.

"What do you have in here, rocks?"

I shrugged. "I brought a few pairs of boots and lots of sweaters."

He laughed. "You really don't know how to pack light."

"And it's really not your problem."

He nudged me with his free hand. "I'm just joking."

"There's mine." Hailey grabbed her bag.

"I could have gotten that for you." Andrew tried to take the bag.

"It's not a problem."

"Okay, if you're sure."

I smiled. Hailey was enjoying his attention, even if she didn't want to show it.

I turned back to Toby. "You can drop my bag."

"I've got it."

"And I'm leaving."

"I'm going with you."

"No you're not. Andrew is not giving you a ride." I gave Andrew a look daring him to argue. He nodded.

Maybe he wasn't as bad as I thought.

"Why don't you let me give you a ride? I'll follow Andrew back to where you're staying. It will give us a chance to talk privately."

"Not a chance." I yanked my bag out of his hand, quickly putting it down so I could roll it. "Let's go." I started walking, hoping Andrew and Hailey would follow.

"Cut me a break, Allie. I left at three in the morning to drive up here."

I turned back to him. "Whose choice was that?"

"How far away are you guys?" Toby asked Andrew.

"About a half hour."

"I think you can handle thirty minutes in the car with me. You've spent a lot more time than that with me before." He gave me his puppy dog look that always broke me.

"And then what? You're going to drop me off and leave."

"If you really want me to."

I turned to Hailey. "I don't want to prolong this. Do you mind if I go with him and we'll follow you?"

"Not if that's what you want."

Andrew grinned. "I'm sure I'll keep Hailey entertained."

I waited as Andrew gave Toby the address of our condo in case we got separated. I hoped that wouldn't be an issue.

We split up when we reached the lot. Hailey pulled me aside to whisper in my ear. "Call me if you need me. I probably shouldn't separate from you, but you seemed to want some time to deal with him."

"I'll be fine. It's just Toby."

"Okay, I'll be ready to talk when we get there."

I hugged her. "Thanks."

"Of course."

Toby opened the back of his silver Acura SUV. He wordlessly picked up my bag and placed it inside, next to his own, before closing it. He followed me to the passenger side and opened my door for me. Toby always insisted on that. When we first started dating it had seemed so charming. By the end, it got annoying.

I buckled up as I waited for him to get in.

He glanced over and smiled at me before typing the address into the GPS. He pulled out of the spot and caught up with Andrew as he paid and left the lot.

"I can't believe you're really here."

"You and me both."

"Your friend seems nice."

"She is. She's awesome." At least Hailey was a safe topic.

"Is she on your floor or something?"

"She's my roommate. We met over the summer."

"Oh, cool." He fidgeted with the radio, finally settling on a classic rock station.

It was obvious the car had been sitting outside for hours, it was freezing. I pulled my pea coat tighter around me, trying to get warm.

"You cold?"

I nodded. I really looked at him for the first time. Nothing about him had actually changed. He still had the same slightly long, brown hair, but he looked different. Almost older somehow.

He reached over and turned on my heated seat. "I would have done that right away, but you're never cold."

"I'm not used to the temperature yet."

"What, a few months down south ruined you?"

"I'm not ruined."

He looked at me. "No, you're not."

I glanced out the window and watched the wintery landscape. It must have recently snowed, because a fresh layer of white coated the grass and trees. "Why are you really here?"

"I already told you. I needed to see you."

"Why? There's nothing left to talk about."

"Of course there is. We need to talk about us." He picked up my left hand in his.

"There is no us—"

"There's an us." He squeezed my hand, and I tried to pull it away.

"Nice ring. You've never been a ring person." His grip on my hand tightened.

I wasn't going to lie. Honesty was probably my only way to get through to Toby. "It's from Levi."

He stiffened. "I'm going to hope you're wearing it on your left hand because it doesn't fit on your right."

"Toby…"

"No. Don't say another word. This is unbelievable." I could almost feel the anger rolling off him. "What are you doing, Allie? You barely know the guy. If you wanted an engagement ring, I would have given you one. Hell, I'd still give you one." He glanced over at me.

I looked out the window.

"No response? No explanation?"

"What do you want me to say?" I finally tugged my hand free. It felt cold.

He shook his head. "This is such a big mistake."

"It's none of your business."

He slammed his hands on the wheel. "Like hell it's none of my business! What happened to us, Allie? We were so happy, and you ended it out of nowhere. Then you leave town and decide to shack up with some random guy. Now you think you're marrying him?"

"Excuse me? First of all, I am not 'shacking up' with anyone. I live in a dorm. Secondly, I don't have to justify my decision to break up with you. We weren't right, and if you'd just think about it, you'd agree."

"I'm never going to agree."

"There are plenty of other girls out there. I'm sure you've found some at Princeton." I crossed my arms.

"Are you asking whether I hooked up with anyone this semester?"

"No. I really don't care. You can sleep with anyone you want."

"Like you mean that. I know you care."

"I don't."

"I'll tell you anyway. I've slept with girls—plenty of them."

"Lovely. Thanks for sharing." I turned away.

He put a hand on my leg, and I looked back at him. "But none of them were you. I only want you."

I pushed Toby's hand off my leg. "You'll find someone, and when you do, you'll realize I made the right decision. You'll know what it really feels like to be in love." My thoughts went to Levi. I missed him already.

"Why are you rushing into marriage? It isn't like you."

"I'm not discussing this with you."

"You're not happy. I can see it on your face."

"I am happy!" I couldn't explain what was really upsetting me.

"No, you're not. And if you'd just give me the chance, I can remind you what it's like to feel happy. And, contrary to what you said, I do know what it's really like to be in love."

"I can't handle this."

"Hiding from me isn't going to help. When are you supposed to get married anyway?"

"This summer." At least that's what Levi's dad thought.

He shifted, pulling his jacket off. "What does your mom think?"

Out of habit, I helped him pull his arm free. He always got hot driving and needed to take his coat off. "She doesn't know."

"You plan on getting married in a few months and your mom doesn't know? You tell your mom everything. That should tell you something."

"We're almost there. Have you said everything you needed to say?" I tried to sound nonchalant, but our conversation shook me up. Being near Toby brought up too many feelings, too many questions. I didn't need any more doubts.

"I haven't come close."

I sighed. "What else is there?"

"I think you should transfer to Princeton. You still have your spot."

"I'm not transferring."

"Why not?"

"Because I like Tulane, and I'm not starting over again."

"It won't be starting completely over. I'm there. I'll introduce you to my friends."

"And all the girls you slept with?" I couldn't resist. I didn't appreciate him forcing images of him with other girls on me. I may have been over him, but I didn't want to think of him that way.

"I actually made you jealous, didn't I?"

"No. Just grossed out. I don't need to know about your man whore ways." I already spent enough time with Jared.

"What if I told you I lied, and I didn't actually sleep with anyone else?"

"I wouldn't care."

"Well, I lied."

"Why?"

"I wanted to make you jealous."

I couldn't help but laugh. "You are so weird."

"Not weird, desperate." He took my hand again. "Please, Allie. Give me another chance? If you'd only seen what a mess I've been."

"Toby, you have to move on."

"I can't. You didn't give me any closure."

"Closure? I told you it was over. What other closure do you want?" I didn't like rubbing salt in his wounds, but he needed to wake up and accept it.

"One more night. Just one more night. I need a chance to say goodbye for real."

I choked. "Are you insane?"

"No. I think it might help both of us."

"And how would that help me?"

"You'd know for sure you were making the right decision."

I freed my hand again. "You really are insane."

"No, just hear me out. If you let me make love to you one more time, and you really don't feel anything, then you'll know you made the right choice. But if you do feel something…then I'd be saving you from making a big mistake." Toby stepped on the brakes as we hit stop-dead traffic.

"Ugh."

"So what do you say? It doesn't have to be tonight…any night you want."

"I have to be on a reality TV show or something. Someone's pranking me, right?"

He laughed. "No. I told you I'm desperate. I had to try."

"I've made up my mind, Toby."

"Break ups aren't fair. Why does only one person have power? We both agreed to start dating. Why do you get to make the decision to end it? Shouldn't it be a joint decision too?"

"Relationships aren't a democracy. Not everyone gets an equal vote."

"I take it you're rejecting my offer."

"Even if we pretended for a second that I wanted to sleep with you, which I don't, I have a boyfriend."

"A boyfriend you didn't bring home with you. A boyfriend your mom doesn't know you plan to marry. Tell me, why didn't you bring him home? Why bring the roommate?"

I hated that he asked. I didn't want him to ask. "It's none of your business."

He groaned. "That can't be your answer to everything."

"It is." We were still in stopped traffic. I noticed Andrew's car two ahead of ours. Without really thinking, I undid my seatbelt. "I gave you your half hour." I opened the door.

"Allie. Are you nuts?"

I didn't answer. I knocked on Hailey's window and Andrew unlocked the door. He turned and smiled at me as I slipped in. "Decided to join us?"

"Well, after Toby asked me to have sex, I wasn't interested in sitting in traffic with him."

Hailey laughed. "Seriously?"

"Completely."

"You really do attract the cocky bastards, don't you?"

"Unfortunately." A knock on my window startled me. Toby peered in with a scowl on his face.

I couldn't believe he'd just leave his car sitting there.

He motioned for me to open my window.

I shook my head.

Thankfully, the traffic started to move, and Toby ran back to his car.

"Unbelievable."

"It's kind of like old times." Andrew looked at me in the rearview mirror. "You guys used to have some pretty crazy fights."

"See, just another reason it's good we broke up."

"You and Levi fight a lot too." Hailey turned to look at me. "Maybe it's just your thing."

"Maybe." I grumbled.

CHAPTER TWENTY-THREE

Mom ran out of the house before I'd even unbuckled. I opened my door, impressed by the exterior of the condo. It was a step up from where we usually stayed. We'd spent quite a few weeks skiing in Vermont when I was growing up, but it had been several years since I'd been back.

"Allie!" The tears spilling down Mom's face reminded me that this had been the longest we'd ever been apart.

"Hi, Mom." I let her pull me out, holding on to her like she might disappear if I let go.

After hugging Mom for a full minute, I finally remembered I wasn't alone. "Mom, this is Hailey."

Hailey smiled, holding out her hand.

Mom ignored her hand and hugged her instead. "Hi, Hailey. It's wonderful to meet such a good friend of Allie's. I'm glad you could join us."

"Thanks for having me." Hailey smiled. "Wow, you two look so alike." She looked between Mom and me.

"They definitely do." That's when I noticed the man behind Mom. "Hi, Allie. It's great to see you."

I wasn't sure if I'd ever met Andrew's dad before. "Hi, Steven." I needed to use his name and stop thinking of him as Andrew's dad. I held out a hand to shake his, but he hugged me instead. It felt awkward but I went with it.

"Hi, Diane. It's lovely to see you again." Toby hugged my very surprised mother.

"Toby? What are you doing here?" She was asking him but looking at me.

I shrugged and rolled my eyes.

"I thought I'd surprise Allie."

"Oh. I bet she was surprised." Mom gave me a sidelong glance.

Toby seemed to have just noticed Steven. "Hi, I'm not sure if we've actually been introduced before. I'm Toby Henderson."

"Hi, Toby. It's nice to see you." He turned to his son. "Andrew, you didn't mention that you and Toby were in touch again."

Andrew sighed. He was probably getting tired of the accusations. "We're not. He was at the airport when I got there."

Steven looked toward Toby, waiting for an explanation.

"I missed Allie so much. I already knew we'd made a mistake when we broke up, and I hoped I could talk some sense into her."

I put a hand on my hip and stared him down "Are you done trying to talk sense into me?"

"No. Not by a long shot."

"I'm going to get my stuff out of your car. Then you can go."

"Allie!" Mom snapped at me. Of course, she'd call me out on being rude. I wonder what she'd think if she knew what he'd suggested in the car.

Mom turned to Toby. "Where are you staying?"

"I haven't found a place yet. I think everything's booked. The only thing on my mind when I left was seeing Allie." He reached over and grabbed my hand. I shrugged him off.

"You drove up here today? What time did you leave?"

Steven asked.

"About three-thirty this morning."

"Oh boy. You're welcome to stay with us, Toby. We have plenty of room." Steven looked at Toby sympathetically. "Now that's what I call dedication." He turned his attention back to me. "Maybe you should give him a chance."

Was Mom's boyfriend, who didn't know me from a hole in the wall, trying to give me dating advice?

"That's really generous of you. I'd love to stay." He smiled at me. "I'll go get our stuff, babe."

Did he really think he could call me that again? I tried not to grimace. He went over to his car and returned a minute later with both of our bags.

Andrew already had Hailey's bag. He wasn't going to let her beat him to the punch again. I had a feeling watching the two of them would be entertaining.

Steven led the way into the house and Mom held back and put an arm around me. "How are you holding up?" she asked quietly.

"I'm surviving."

Steven walked into the main room. A couple of comfortable looking couches and chairs surrounded a large fireplace that wasn't currently lit. A kitchen was off to one side and there were two small hallways. Mom removed her arm and waited with Steven in the kitchen. The rest of us followed Andrew down the second hallway. He stopped in front of one of the two doorways.

"I guess you're staying with me, Toby." He gestured into a room with a set of bunk beds.

"We're next door?" Hailey asked.

"Yup. Diane figured you guys would rather share a queen than have bunk beds."

"She was right." I walked into our room and tossed my purse and coat on the dresser.

Hailey did the same. "This is nice."

***

"Tell me everything." Mom put an arm around my shoulder as we curled up with blankets on a couch in front of the fire. Hailey decided to take a nap while the guys went to the store to pick up some food for dinner. I was relieved when Toby accepted Steven's offer to go. I needed time with Mom.

"About…" I knew exactly what she meant, but I wasn't ready to face it yet.

"Let's start with the ring." She picked up my hand, taking a closer look at the ruby ring.

"Yeah, the ring."

"It's from Levi, isn't it?"

I wasn't going to lie. I'd never been good at lying to my mother. "Yes."

"When were you going to tell me?"

"It's not what you think…" I leaned back against the couch.

"Then explain it."

If only I could. "It's complicated."

"Complicated, huh? Okay, let's start simple. Are you and Levi engaged?" She put a hand on my arm.

I dared to glance at her. "Kind of."

"Come on, Allie, be straight with me. How can you be 'kind of' engaged?"

I wanted to spill it all out. "It means we are, but I'm not sure if I want it."

Those words must have had some magical quality, because her tough exterior melted and she pulled me into her arms. "Oh, honey."

I let her hold me, loving the comforting feel of her and the familiar scent of her perfume.

"This is because of your father and me, isn't it?"

I looked up at her. "What?"

"We didn't give you a positive view of marriage, and I spent your entire childhood telling you how big a mistake

226

it is to get married young. But if you love Levi—"

"This isn't about you and Dad." I wasn't letting her blame herself for any of this.

"Do you love him?"

"Yes." At least I could answer that honestly.

She smiled. "Well, that's a start. You're young. If you're not ready, you're not ready. I just don't want you making a decision based on what happened to me."

"I'm not." I looked her right in the eye.

"If you weren't sure, why'd you take the ring?" She asked it quietly, like she was afraid of upsetting me.

"I didn't have a choice." I whispered it, not sure whether I wanted her to hear it.

She pursed her lips, and I knew she was choosing her words carefully. "Because you were afraid you'd lose Levi otherwise?"

I didn't say anything.

"I had no idea he was so serious about your relationship." She rubbed my back the way she always did when I was upset. "Does he make you happy?"

I shrugged. "Most of the time."

She laughed. "Fair enough."

"I'm not going to tell you what to do. You're an adult. I knew you had strong feelings for him when you decided to stay in New Orleans. You tried to tell me it wasn't about him, but obviously I was right."

I nodded.

"Did you invite him to come here with you?"

"No. He wanted to, but I needed space to think, you know?"

"I know. I'll try not to push you too much, sweetie, but I just want you to do the best thing for yourself. When I visited you this summer, I tried to encourage you to take chances, but don't confuse that with turning your back on who you are."

"I won't." I didn't know if I could keep my word, but I'd try.

"We're home," Steven called from the front hallway.

"Coming." Mom patted my leg before getting up. "You'll be okay no matter what you decide."

"Thanks, Mom."

"Where's Hailey?" Andrew asked, coming to sit down next to me on the couch.

"Sleeping."

He looked over his shoulder, probably making sure she wasn't suddenly coming out of her room. "Is she single?"

I laughed. "Yes, but don't get your hopes up."

"Why not?"

I decided to be nice. "Because we're only here for a week."

He visibly relaxed. "It's a whole week."

"If you say so."

His expression grew serious. "Are you really engaged?"

I nodded. "Toby told you?"

"Yeah. My dad asked why he didn't just give you more space."

"Oh." I didn't know what else to say.

Andrew didn't respond right away. Then he cleared his throat. "Why are you engaged? Don't you think you're too young? This just doesn't seem like you."

I turned toward him. "Since when do you know anything about me?"

"We've gone to school together forever."

"Until this year."

"And you've changed that much in a few months?"

"Does this conversation have a purpose?" I didn't want to start a fight, but I didn't know how much more I could take.

"I just think you should check out all your options."

"My options?"

"I don't mean me. Obviously, that's out of the question now that we're probably going to be family, but there are tons of other guys."

"Toby didn't put you up to this, did he?"

"No. You know we're not friends. I was glad when I heard you kicked him to the curb. He never deserved you."

Maybe I needed to reevaluate my feelings about Andrew.

"How long have you known this other guy, Lyle is it?"

"Levi."

"Levi? Like the jeans?"

"I guess. It's short for Leviathan. And I've known him six months."

"So you really just met him this summer? Doesn't this seem rushed?" Andrew seemed genuinely concerned so I didn't snap at him.

"He's someone who knows what he wants."

"My dad thinks you're making a mistake. He's going to talk to your mom about it."

"Great." I felt anger rising. Who did Steven think he was to butt in?

"Hey." Toby walked in and sat down right next to me. "Am I interrupting something?"

"Not really. I'm just trying to figure out why Allie's rushing to get married." Andrew paused and then made a strange face. "Wait, you're not pregnant are you?"

"No!"

"Okay, just checking."

I crossed my arms. "People get married young for reasons other than pregnancy."

Toby smiled at me condescendingly. "What reasons do you have?"

"I don't have to answer that. Now if you'll excuse me, I'm going to wake up Hailey. If she sleeps much more, she'll be up all night."

I escaped into the bedroom, closing the door behind me. I hoped Toby left in the morning. I wasn't sure how much more I could take.

The sun had disappeared, leaving the room dark. I turned on a lamp and collapsed on my side of the bed. I fished my cell out of my bag. I had a missed text from

Levi.

I miss you already. When are you coming home?

He already knew the answer, but I told him anyway. *In a week.* I pressed send and then decided to send another one. *I miss you too.*

Good. You should miss me.

At least I could rely on Levi being his cocky self.

***

I couldn't sleep. I tossed and turned for hours, unable to quiet my racing mind. All of my confusion over what to do with Levi was made ten times worse after seeing Toby. It's not that I wanted to get back with him—not at all—but he brought back so many memories and reminded me about my dreams and the life I left behind.

By one a.m., I'd had enough. I pulled on jeans and my coat and headed outside to get some fresh air. I took a seat on an Adirondack chair, wondering if I was being watched. I was positive Levi had covered all the security bases. I tried to sit, but I was too antsy. I got up and walked out onto the snow covered grass. The moon was full and beautiful.

The wind picked up, bringing the start of some snow flurries with it, and I pulled my coat tightly around me. I really needed to build my cold tolerance up again.

"You couldn't sleep either?"

I didn't need to turn around to know it was Toby. I'd never forget his voice. I'd dated lots of boys before him, but he was the first one that I ever let in.

"No. I got tired of tossing and turning."

"Same here. It was hard knowing you were just on the other side of the wall."

I turned to look at him. "I'm sorry."

"For?" He studied my face intently.

"Hurting you."

"You did what you thought you had to."

"I did have to. I still know it was the best thing for both of us."

He moved closer. "I still know that it wasn't—for either of us. I don't want to keep fighting with you, but I know we're perfect together."

"What does perfect even mean?" Without thinking, I brushed some snow out of Toby's hair.

"Shouldn't you know? You're the one getting married."

I looked away. "I don't think anything can be perfect."

"Sure it can. Perfect is when you're with someone who completes you in every way: emotionally, physically, sexually…"

"But what does it mean to complete you? Can you be complete but still feel confused?" I probably shouldn't have been so honest with Toby, but it was late, and I was used to being open with him.

"What are you confused about?" He moved so close I could feel his body heat. I'd forgotten how warm he ran. He was just like Levi in that way.

"Everything, but mostly what I want out of life. Sometimes I feel like I don't even know myself anymore. It's like life started moving forward so quickly, and now I can't slow it down."

Toby wiped away some tears that had slipped out. "It's going to be okay, Allie."

"You can't say that. You have no idea what's been happening."

"I want to know. I want to help." He pulled me into a hug, and I let him hold me. Maybe it was selfish, but I needed to be held. Without it, I might have unraveled completely. I tried to be strong, but sometimes I felt so weak.

I started to cry. Toby just held me, rubbing my back gently as I sobbed.

I finally composed myself enough to pull away. "I'm sorry."

"Why are you sorry this time?"

"For breaking down. You know that's not like me."

"Yes. I do know that, because I know you. Whatever's going on, I can help you. Maybe we can call Princeton this week and get your registration in order."

"I'm not transferring, Toby."

"I'm not asking you to do it for me this time. You said it yourself. Life's out of control. But you're wrong. You can put on the brakes."

"You don't understand. I can't." I ran a finger over my ring.

"If he loves you, he'll understand. He'll get that you aren't ready for something like that."

"I can't just give his ring back." For once, I didn't mean it physically. I knew that I couldn't give it back. Too much had happened since he gave it to me.

"You can do anything you want to do. Anyone who tells you otherwise is wrong."

He took my hand. "Your hands are freezing. You should probably get back inside."

"Probably. It's late." The snow had picked up, and my light-weight wool coat wasn't designed for it.

"I know you didn't want to see me, but I'm not leaving tomorrow."

I was too tired and emotionally spent to argue. "Thanks for being here for me tonight."

He took my other hand. "I want to be there for you every night. I love you, Allie."

"Goodnight." I pulled my hands away and walked inside.

"Goodnight," he called, making no move to follow me inside.

CHAPTER TWENTY-FOUR

After an early breakfast, Hailey and I stopped by the rental shop to pick out our gear before hitting the slopes. It was funny watching Hailey learn about skis for the first time. I was used to her knowing everything. I was giving her a hard time about it when an attractive guy, probably in his mid-twenties, walked over.

"Hi. I couldn't help but overhear that you'd never been skiing before."

Hailey smiled. "Yeah, it's my first time."

"I'm an instructor here. I'd love to give you lessons, if you're interested."

Hailey glanced at me and grinned. "That sounds nice, but I think I'll be fine."

"Are you positive? I'm sure your friend will help, but she isn't actually trained."

"Oh, I'm not relying on Allie. I think I'll figure it out."

He looked taken aback. "Okay. Have fun then."

"We will." I paid for our gear, and we headed out.

"So do you think I should start on the easy ones, or what?"

"I bet you can handle a blue slope."

"I have no idea what that is, but that's fine."

I grabbed her arm through her parka. "Let's go." We got in line for the ski lift.

"I've always wanted to ride a ski lift." Hailey looked all around in excitement.

"Seriously? You can fly, and you've always wanted to sit on a ski lift?"

"It always looks fun in the movies."

I laughed. "All right. Let's go live your dream."

"Hey, I don't make fun of you when you get all dumbstruck over Pteron stuff."

"You don't?" I gave her a skeptical look.

"Okay. Maybe I do."

We waited for our turn and got on a lift next to a young couple. Hailey was all giddy next to me, and it rubbed off. I always liked skiing, but it wasn't my favorite activity.

As I expected, Hailey was incredible. After a few runs, she looked like a pro. We decided to try a black diamond. Everything was fine until I fell halfway down the run after slipping on some moguls. I got back up and made it down, but my right ankle was in pretty bad shape. I could feel the swelling beginning, and I knew I should probably get some ice on it soon.

"Are you okay?" Hailey was at my side as soon as I caught up with her.

"Yeah. I can't believe I'm the one who fell." I rubbed my ankle.

"Beginner's luck."

"Yeah, right."

She held up her hands. "It sounds nice. I'm guessing this means we're done for the day?"

"No. You can stay. I'll take the shuttle back."

"I can't let you go alone."

"I'll be fine. Besides, I'm sure there's someone watching us. Do you really think Levi left my safety to just you, no offense."

"No offense taken. There are some locals watching, and I know Levi sent a few guys up. But they're supposed to stay back."

"I figured that much."

She held out a hand to help me up. "I'll just make sure you get home okay."

"Hail, you're supposed to be having fun."

"I can come back out."

I leaned on her shoulder, trying to keep my weight off the bad ankle. "I'm holding you to it."

We took the shuttle back, and Hailey made sure I had everything I could possibly need before leaving. She really was an awesome friend.

I sat and read for a while before deciding to change into a black bikini to check out the hot tub. We shared it with the next couple of condos, but I doubted anyone else was around. Unless you were a klutz like me, you'd be on the slopes. I slipped into the warm water, hoping it would make my ankle feel better. I closed my eyes and tried to relax.

"Mind if I join you?"

I jumped, surprised that anyone else was home. "Uh, sure." I tried to avoid staring at Toby for too long. He was wearing only a pair of swim trunks and seeing him without a shirt brought back memories. He must have been freezing.

He sat down directly across from me. "How's your ankle?"

"How'd you know about my ankle?"

"We ran into Hailey. Andrew decided to stay back with her." A slow smile spread across his lips. "He was more than happy to see me leave."

I laughed. "I bet. I can't blame him. He isn't the first."

"I'm sure. You probably know something about that too."

"About what?"

"Having lots of people want you."

"Very funny."

"It's true."

I didn't answer. I concentrated on swirling the water around with my hand.

"You look so good in a bikini."

"Thanks."

"I mean it. I have a picture of you wearing that white bikini you had the summer before senior year. Let's just say I look at it a lot." He wriggled an eyebrow.

"Get rid of that picture. It's time to move on." Despite our conversation the night before, I was determined to make Toby realize he needed to let go.

"I'm not getting rid of it. It's a nice memory."

"Memories imply something in the past. Let go."

"I'm not ready to let go." His lips were on mine before I'd even processed he'd moved across the hot tub. His arms wrapped around me in a vice grip. The kiss felt good—sweet, familiar, comforting. It was a kiss I knew well, but it was nothing like the fireworks I felt with Levi. It was wrong, completely wrong, and I had to get out of the situation. I pushed against him as hard as I could, but he didn't budge. I moved my knee, ready to get him where it hurt when he let go and moved back. "You felt something, right?"

I shook my head. "Try that again and you'll regret it." I got out and wrapped myself in a towel.

"I won't regret it." He smirked. "And I know you felt it. You responded to me."

I moved inside quickly and jumped in the shower, washing off every ounce of Toby. It felt so wrong. I felt so wrong. I hadn't wanted him to kiss me, but maybe I'd let it happen. Either way, I needed to see Levi. I got out of the shower and got dressed. I blow dried my hair, wanting every excuse possible to stay in my room until Hailey or my mom came back.

Finally, Hailey came into the room. "Hey, how's the ankle?"

"The ankle's fine, but we have to go home."

"Home? As in to New Orleans?" I saw the excitement in her eyes. I knew she was having fun on our trip, but she missed New Orleans. The cold was never quite her thing.

"I need to see Levi."

"Are you okay?"

"Yes, I just need to see him." I paced the room, wanting to leave immediately.

"Should we look for flights?"

"Can't you fly us?"

Hailey laughed. "You must really want to see him, but I think we can take a commercial airline."

"Fine. I hope my mom gets back soon."

I waited until I saw my Mom alone that evening to break the news. "Mom, can we talk?"

"Sure." She picked up a blanket and walked out onto the back porch. I tried not to look at the hot tub. "Is something wrong?"

"I need to go back to New Orleans."

"You miss him, don't you?" She smiled.

"Yes. And I need him to know how I feel."

"I don't want you to leave, but I know love when I see it."

"You'll forgive me?" I felt terrible that I was leaving right after I got there, but somehow I knew she'd understand.

"Of course, but maybe you can make a trip home after the New Year?"

"Yes. I'll bring Levi."

"Good. I need to get to know him better."

I leaned over and hugged her. "I love you, Mom."

"I love you too."

CHAPTER TWENTY-FIVE

"Al?" Levi answered the door, evidently surprised to see me on the other side.

I took advantage of his surprise, launching myself at him. I wrapped my arms around his waist and leaned my head on his chest.

"Is everyone okay? What's going on?"

I looked up into the blue-gray eyes that had me at first glance. "I love you, Levi."

He grinned. "I love you too, Al."

I leaned up to kiss him, loving how quickly he responded and how incredible it felt. I was right—what I had with Levi went beyond simple attraction. I'd never find anything even remotely close to it. He lifted me up, carrying me to his bedroom. He kicked his door closed before laying me down on his bed.

"We're leaving," Jared yelled, and I heard the front door slam. I was glad. I knew Pterons had good hearing, and I didn't want to have to worry about being quiet. I didn't want to worry about anything but being with Levi.

I pulled Levi's head down, wanting his lips on mine again. He moved back after a minute, pulling off my sweater and his shirt. "I've been waiting to get you naked in my bed for a long time, and I'm not wasting a second."

"I don't want to waste any time either."

"Good." He unbuttoned my jeans and slid them off. "Red panties? Were these intentional?"

I shrugged. "Maybe subconsciously."

He took off his pants, and returned to unclasp my bra. His mouth moved to claim my breast.

"I like the red, but I like you naked better." He took off my panties, and I reached out to grab him as he leaned over me again.

I was barely aware of him lifting me enough to pull down his covers. His hands and lips touched me everywhere before he positioned himself over me. "I love you. Every single part of you."

I smiled. "Then show me."

***

"I don't know what caused it, but if this is what's going to happen when you go on vacation, you should go more often."

"Next time, you should come with me." I meant it.

He smiled, running a hand down my stomach underneath the covers. "I like that idea."

I curled up against him, our bodies tangled together in the sheet. "Your bed is pretty comfortable."

"Comfortable enough you're going to spend all of your nights here?"

"Not all, but a lot."

"That's a good start." His lips brushed against my neck.

My phone rang, ruining the moment. I tried to push Levi off so I could see who was calling.

"Ignore it."

I started to sit up. "Let me see who it is."

"No." He pushed me back down.

I was all about going along with it until my phone rang

again. "Give me my purse."

"Fine."

He handed it to me, but not fast enough to avoid the call going to voice mail. I looked at my phone. I had two missed calls from Jess. It was weird that she'd called twice without leaving a message.

"I have to call her back." I pulled the sheet tightly around me, feeling strange calling her while naked in bed with Levi.

He made it a little less awkward. "Fine, I'm going to make us something to eat. Don't go anywhere. I'll bring it back here."

"Okay," I said absently as he left the room.

"Hello, Allie," a male voice answered.

I froze. I recognized that voice, and it wasn't Emmett.

"Allie, help please!" I heard Jess scream in the background.

"What the hell is going on?"

"I told you to come back to me, but you wouldn't listen."

My stomach dropped. "Toby, please, what's going on? Why do you have Jess?"

"You want Jess? Agree to come back to me. That's all it will take."

"Answer me. Why do you have her?"

"You really don't get it, do you? We are meant to be together, but you are too blinded to realize it."

"Have you lost your mind?"

"No, but you have. All it takes is a pair of wings to get you in bed, huh?"

"What?" Had he just said what I thought he did?

He laughed. "I'm surprised you haven't figured it out yet. I thought you were smarter than that."

"Figured what out? How did you know about his wings?"

"I guess I never mentioned my mother's maiden name, did I?"

Toby's mother had been dead since he was a kid. I had no reason to know it. "No, why?"

"Does Blackwell ring a bell?" My chest clenched. "Are the pieces falling into place, babe?"

If I hadn't been sitting down, I would have collapsed. "Wait are you... you can't be."

"I can't? Why not?"

"Because it's impossible. How could I have been with two... this makes no sense."

"Why not? Are Levi and I really that different?"

"But why? And if you wanted me, why not just get me while I was there?"

"They still haven't told you how much power you have, have they?" Toby laughed dryly. "If you want Jess back, you'll come to me willingly. I can almost handle knowing he's had his hands on you since it's going to make things even better for us. I promised I could take care of everything, and I never break my promises. I know you think you can't leave him, but you can, and you will."

"Toby? Please."

"I'll be in touch, and when I am, you're going to come to me." The line went dead.

Levi walked in and found me holding the phone in shock.

"Al, what's wrong?"

"They have Jess."

"Who does?" He sat down on the bed next to me.

"The Blackwells."

"The Blackwells? Who called you?" He put a hand on my back.

"Toby. He says he's a Pteron. A Blackwell."

"Your ex-boyfriend?"

"Levi, why did he say he needs me to come willingly?"

Levi's face paled. "It doesn't matter. You're not going to him."

I shook off my annoyance that he was evading my question again. "We have to get Jess back. I'll do whatever

I have to. I can't let anyone else get hurt because of me."

"We'll get her back, but you're not going anywhere."

Levi pulled me against him, and I knew that I'd save Jess even if I had to do it alone.

Keep reading for a preview of **Found (The Crescent Chronicles #3)**. For more information about Alyssa Rose Ivy's books, please visit her online at:

www.AlyssaRoseIvy.com
www.facebook.com/AlyssaRoseIvy
twitter.com/AlyssaRoseIvy
AlyssaRoseIvy@gmail.com
To stay up to date on Alyssa's new releases, join her
mailing list: http://eepurl.com/ktlSj

FOUND
the
crescent chronicles

CHAPTER ONE

If Levi mentioned my sex life with Toby one more time I was going to slap him.

"I don't see how it changes anything. You already knew I wasn't a virgin."

"I thought you'd been with a human. That's different. Human men don't count. I assumed I was your first Pteron." The serious expression on his face made me want to laugh despite my anger.

"That's ridiculous." I tied the laces on my running shoes. I was antsy from spending so much time inside and was excited that Hailey was coming by Levi's house to meet me for a run.

"It was nothing like it is with us, right? Just tell me that."

I let out a deep breath. "How many human girls were you with before me?"

"Uh—"

"Yeah, I thought so. Does that mean what we have isn't special? Different?"

"Of course not." He sat down next to me, leaving no space between us. "Those girls meant nothing. You mean everything."

"Exactly." I decided not to berate him about the disrespectful way he treated women before me. "You may not have been my first Pteron, but you're my favorite." I kissed him on the cheek. I was trying to pretend it didn't weird me out, but I was going crazy. How was it possible for me to have been with two different Pterons? I wasn't even nineteen yet.

His shoulder brushed against mine. "Have we had sex more times than you guys did?"

"What?" I shot up and away from him. "No. No. No. We are not talking about this anymore. Say it again and you can forget about us having sex any time in the near future. Got it?"

He put up his hands in mock defense. "Fine. I just don't like it."

"You've made your feelings abundantly clear." I turned to walk out of his bedroom to wait for Hailey. I didn't make it through the doorway.

His arms wrapped around my waist and pulled me back against him. "How long do you have before Hailey gets here?" He kissed my earlobe before trailing a line of kisses down my neck.

"Not enough time." I spun out of his arms. "I wouldn't want to cut your amazing skills short."

He laughed. "Just wait until tonight, Al. I'll show you amazing."

"I can hardly wait." I leaned up and kissed him. I should have known it wouldn't be just a quick little kiss. He wasn't having any of that. He had me pinned against the wall within seconds. My hands were tangled in his hair almost as quickly.

That was exactly how Hailey found us. "I'd tell you to get a room, but I guess you already have one."

Levi reluctantly backed up. "Impeccable timing as always, Hailey."

She shrugged. "What can I say? I have the touch."

"That you do. Let's get out of here." I ran a finger down Levi's bare arm. "Don't get too bored without me."

"I probably will. See you girls later." He waved.

We stopped on the porch to stretch before taking off running down the block. We cut over to St. Charles Avenue to run the street car line. Hailey had to try hard to run slow enough for me to keep pace. If you want an inferiority complex, spend all of your time with paranormal creatures.

"Do you know what you're wearing tonight?" Hailey asked.

"I'm going to wear that red strapless dress I picked out with you a few months ago." We were going to a paranormal New Year's Eve party. I figured a short, sexy dress worked no matter what kind of party it was. I wasn't thrilled about going, considering how worried I was about Jess, but the deeper I could get into Society events, the better chance I had at finding out how to get her back.

Hailey laughed. "Trying to make Levi's night, huh?"

"Why not? Maybe it will make him shut his mouth about Toby."

"It's crazy though, isn't it?" She sped up again, forcing me to push myself harder to keep up.

I watched her red ponytail bobbing in front of me. "Definitely. I just wish I knew how it was possible. It can't be a coincidence."

"You think there's more to it? Like what, you're a Pteron magnet or something?"

"A Pteron magnet? Those exist?" I barely got the words out. I was already out of breath.

"Of course not." Hailey turned, running backwards. "I thought you've been training with the guys."

I stuck my tongue out at her. It was childish, but she deserved it. "Sorry, we aren't all as fast as you."

"I'm only running at half speed."

"Remind me again why we're friends?" I finally gave up. I stopped and bent over, clutching my knees.

"Because you love me." She stopped too.

"Do you love me enough to carry me home?"

"No, but he does."

I didn't need to turn around to know that Levi was behind us. "Normally I'd get mad at you for following us, but right now I don't care."

I turned and let him pull me into a hug—a sweaty hug. I was the only one who was sweaty. He was perfectly dry in his black running shirt and gray shorts. He always looked good in gym clothes.

"Do you really need me to carry you?" His tone was hopeful.

"It's tempting, but I'm going to keep going. Think you can walk next to me or something? That would probably be the right pace."

Hailey sighed. "I can try again. I really did try."

I smiled. "It's okay, Hail. Go on ahead."

"See you guys in a few." She disappeared down the street.

I gave myself another few seconds to recover. "Ready, favorite Pteron of mine?"

"Always." Levi didn't actually walk, it was more like a jog. It probably took effort to go so slow, but he didn't seem to mind. I'd only been back from Vermont a few days, and I don't think he wanted to let me out of his sight. A week before it would have annoyed me. But after learning about Jess's kidnapping, I didn't mind the extra protection.

"Did Jared find out anything else?" With Bryant locked up in The Society equivalent of a prison, Jared had moved up the chain. Although he wouldn't be a full-fledged security officer until after graduation, he was in on all of the decision making.

"Not really. She's still being kept in that house, but she's unharmed. I promise you, she's going to be okay. If we thought otherwise, we'd go in and get her. It's just not worth tipping the Blackwells off about our inside man yet. We need to find out more before you and your friends are safe."

"Is Emmett still there?" The only thing keeping me remotely calm was finding out that Jess' boyfriend was with her.

"Yes. They're going to be okay."

"I hope so. I feel awful."

"Don't."

"You make it sound so easy. My best friend's been kidnapped because of me."

"We'll get her back, Al. I promise."

I tried to smile, but it wasn't easy. I knew she wasn't being hurt, but she was still being denied freedom. I also had no idea what would happen when Toby found out I wasn't going to him. What if he took it out on her?

"Ready to turn around, or do you want to keep going?" He gestured further down the street.

"Let's head back. Hailey wore me out."

He laughed. "Sounds good. Since you're so tired, you'll need my help in the shower."

"Your willingness to help astounds me sometimes."

He grinned. "It's so good to have you home."

"You do realize I'm moving back into my dorm when it opens, right?"

"We'll see." There was a twinkle in his eye that let me know he wasn't buying it.

I let it go. I was sure we'd have plenty of time to argue about it later.

Found is available now!

CPSIA information can be obtained at www.ICGtesting.com
Printed in the USA
BVOW02s1804020614

355176BV00005B/268/P